To Kat

Beautifully
Wounded

Hugs,
Sue Briscom
xoxo

To Kristen,

Hugs,
xoxo

Beautifully Wounded

Susan Griscom

Amber Glow Books

Formally published as The Fawn
Amber Glow Books
AmberGlowBooks.com
www.susangriscom.com

Edited by Michael Leah Olson
Cover designed by Susan Griscom

ISBN-13: 978-1497596139 (Paperback)
ISBN-10: 1497596130

Other works by Susan Griscom

The Whisper Cape Series
Whisper Cape, Book 1
Reflections, Book 2
A Secret Fate, Book 3

Also by Susan Griscom
Allusive Aftershock (A young adult novel, 2013)
Brief Interludes (A collection of short stories with a twist)
Erotic Interludes (An anthology by S.M. Griscom & Anabel Blue)

Coming summer 2014
Book Two of The Beaumont Brothers, Brodie's Story (New Adult Contemporary Romance)

Beautifully Wounded

Chapter 1

Lena

*H*e opened the front door. Rusty hinges creaked in the otherwise stillness of the night as he entered our dark, two-story home. No one could have slept through the sound of the door slamming behind him, or the thump of his footsteps on the stairs as I pictured him lumbering his way up to the bedroom where I supposedly slept. He swore with dissonance, and every bone in my body stiffened as I squeezed my eyes so tight they hurt. When a thump, followed by a clang resonated through the house, I visualized a picture crashing to the floor, glass shattering as it toppled to the bottom of the steps—the one and only picture of us on our wedding day, no doubt. Troy was drunk, again. I knew he would be—

1

knew it when he left earlier that evening. I'd come to learn it was an ugly habit with him most nights. I stared up at the dingy white ceiling of our darkened bedroom, tainted with water stains from a leaky roof. A sliver of light from the street lamp peeked through the window and illuminated a slender line across the wall. I stayed still as a corpse, breathing shallow and praying he was drunk enough to just pass out.

My body involuntarily stiffened when he tumbled on top of me, groping at my breasts, forcing his hard slobbering lips against mine. I forced myself to go limp; my rigid body would only make him mad. I stopped breathing for as long as I could to ward off the stink of booze and cigarettes emanating from his pores and from his hot, sour breath. A vile tincture accumulated in my throat and I fought back the urge to vomit.

Don't get me wrong, it wasn't always like this. There was a time I enjoyed being with Troy, when making love was something special, something exciting. But not now, not like this. There would be no titillating foreplay here, no show of affection. Not from him, that wasn't his style, at least not anymore. His style was brutal, self-serving, and revolting.

I tried not to flinch or look surprised as he ripped my thin nightgown down the front, exposing one of my breasts. Any show of negative emotion might set him off in the wrong direction.

"Get rid of this fucking thing." The demand slurred from his throat. With a sickening laugh, he tugged the cotton away from my body and tossed the shredded material to the floor. There was no point in refusing him. That was something I'd learned the hard way. My face would fare better if I just surrendered to his disgusting sexual assaults.

My underpants were next to endure his rough, impatient hands as he tugged them down over my feet. I doubt they even made it to the floor. They'd become lost somewhere in the sheets.

There used to be a gentle, caring man behind those dark blue eyes—so blue they always reminded me of what I thought the deepest part of the ocean looked like. Now, I only thought of the darkest part of hell—where the fire burned everything to black embers before it moved on.

He stood up, fumbled with his zipper, and stumbled while pushing his pants down. I lie there naked, trying my best not to shiver or show fear, trying so, so hard to keep the tears from flowing. I didn't dare move, didn't dare look at him. I ordered myself to lie still—to make my mind go somewhere else—then I could tolerate the loveless act that was about to happen, as I'd done so many times before. I searched my mind for that time not too long ago when sex with this man was welcomed, a time when I felt special and loved. Oh, I still felt special—a special kind of punching bag if I didn't do what he told me to do.

He practically fell on top of me, the length of his body smothering mine. Stillness forced on me, I ordered myself not to cry out from his heavy weight, knowing any type of complaint would make him violent. The fact that I couldn't seem to take in a full breath of air helped keep me quiet.

"Now, that's better. Oh, yeah, baby," he groaned in my ear, slurping wet, boozy lips down my throat as he shoved his not quite hard erection into me, rocking back and forth.

It amazed me that he could even get the tip inside. The smell of booze on his breath tonight was heavy, and I wondered if he'd finish before he grew frustrated and angry.

It didn't take long for his fury to escalate into blind rage. Cursing, blaming me for not arousing him enough. "You frigid bitch! Show me some affection you stupid cunt!" In his outrage, he backhanded me across the face.

I shouldn't have been surprised, but I always was. I didn't cry out, didn't shed a tear. I'd become numb, I think, because if I did cry or scream, he'd only beat me more and yell at me to shut up. However, this time, I found my apathetic response wouldn't work either. He slapped me again and then dragged me up by my hair, tossing me to the floor. "Get out of my bed you worthless slut. Who you been fucking so you don't want me anymore? You have somebody better than me out there?"

I was too stunned to answer, so he kept on shouting, "Right, ain't nobody gonna wanna fuck an old has-been like you."

It didn't matter that I was only twenty. My body

and my spirit were broken beyond repair, damaged, and I felt as old as his accusations. He stood staggering over me and laughed, one foot on either side of my legs for balance as he reached for himself. I honestly thought he would urinate on me just to show how little he thought of me. He'd done it before, and said I wasn't even worth the piss of a dog. But luckily, this time he just grabbed both my arms and yanked my limp body to my feet.

"You think you can get a better lay than me? You're mistaken. Nobody else will have you. Nobody else wants you. You're a stinking dirty whore! That's what you are."

In the past, I would have begged him to stop, but these days my mind numbed more and more with each assault. It wouldn't make any difference if I answered him or not, it would always be the *wrong* answer. Staying silent was safer. It made him mad, but it didn't give him any more ammunition. Usually.

He laughed again before spitting in my face, and then I felt the bone of his knuckles crack against my upper cheek—or was that my bone that cracked? Then he threw me against the wall. The back of my head slammed against it, and a traitorous groan escaped from my throat as I collapsed. This time, I thought, he just might kill me. He kicked me in the stomach, and again in my side, before he staggered away to the bathroom. I wasn't sure which hurt more: my face, my stomach, or my ribs.

The sound of him urinating gave me reprieve from his wrath, and I decided to try to make a run for it. I honestly didn't know if I'd even make it down the stairs, but I had to try. My legs shook, and every inch of my body ached. I made it to the top of the stairway and had a death grip on the railing for fear I would lose my balance and tumble down the long staircase. The hallway behind me, as well as the stairwell before me, seemed almost invisible in the darkness since Troy hadn't bothered to turn on the lights before staggering upstairs. I didn't even try to locate the switch to illuminate my way. I'd take my chances in the dark, not wanting to alert him to my whereabouts. Barely able to stand, I stumbled my way down to the small kitchen.

I struggled to find the strength to stay on my feet and gripped the counter, leaning against it for support.

"Lena, where the fuck did you go?" he called out as his heavy flat feet thumped down the stairs.

Panic clouded my mind. I needed to get out of there. If he found me standing here, he would surely kill me for not staying put.

I'd saved money, but as I looked down at my naked body I knew I couldn't just run out the door. If he caught up with me, the jealous rage at the sight of my naked body outside would only send him into an even angrier fit. And I couldn't leave without my stash of money.

I glanced around the kitchen. The white laminate counters bare and neat, not even a knickknack or speck of dirt on them per his strict rules. I could have grabbed a heavy pan and hit him over the head, but I didn't think I could walk across the room to where we stored them in time, and quite frankly, I didn't have the strength to wield a heavy enough blow to knock him out. I turned, still grasping the counter, and yanked open the drawer beside the sink. My fingers latched on to one of the small steak knives as he called out again, startling me, his voice not far away. Panic rose, and the rush of adrenalin secreted into my veins as I clutched the knife tightly in my fist. The solid weight of the black plastic handle in my grip felt reassuring, yet terrifying. I ran my fingers down the sharp edge of the blade with my other hand, feeling the jagged edges. My body seemed to move in a dream state or a B-rated horror movie—waiting for the serial killer to come closer—close enough for me to plunge the blade into him. Did I have the courage to do it? If I didn't, he would kill me. He rounded the corner as I turned back around, my shaky hand hiding the blade behind my back.

He weaved his way across the room, his hands fanned out to his sides as if to embrace me, his head cocked to one side, a slight curve to his lips; a rare attempt at a tender gesture.

"Come on, Lena. I'm sorry. Let me make it up to you." His sudden mood swing didn't surprise me. I knew it was just an act to get closer to me so I would let my guard down, then he could strike me again or get close enough to choke me to death.

I didn't move though. Couldn't move. My arms were still behind my back, one clutching the counter for support, the other around that black plastic handle. His hands groped my shoulders and he squeezed his fingers against my skin.

"You shouldn't have left the bedroom, Lena. Now I'll need to punish you." His body wavered and he studied me with bloodshot eyes as if deciding what to do.

Shove it in, my mind demanded, as rage simmered behind those blue eyes. Then his fingers moved to my throat, squeezing tighter and tighter until I couldn't breathe. I closed my eyes, gritted my teeth and pulled the knife around. I thrust it into his gut in the same manner as he had thrust into me a few moments before, cold and brutal. Only I added passion—a passion of hate.

His warm blood oozed over my knuckles. He appeared shocked that I had actually stabbed him. I let go of the handle, leaving the blade stuck in his abdomen.

He gazed at me with wide, shocked eyes. "Lena? Baby, why?" He clutched at his stomach where the plastic stuck out. Blood oozed between his fingers and stained his white shirt. Then his knees buckled and he sank to the floor. "You fucking bitch, I'll kill you for this."

Chapter 2
Lena

I stood rigid as a pole before I realized what I'd done. He fell onto his side, his hands covered in blood, a pool of red spreading under him.

Willing my legs to move, I shuffled my way around him and then ran. I snatched my purse that hung from the closet door handle and grabbed a coat from the coat rack by the door. I shrugged it on as I ran out, stopping only briefly to run to the side of the house and dig up the money I had buried in the ground about five inches under a small boulder.

I grabbed the keys from my purse and ran to the SUV. I didn't even think about where I would go, I just started the car and shoved it in reverse. I fishtailed out of the driveway after turning the car around and spinning the tires as I tore out onto the street. I raced down the interstate heading south out of Medford. I had no particular destination in mind. I didn't care. Tears soaked the collar of my coat as they dripped from my cheeks. As I swiped at them, I wondered how I could possibly have any left. I'd thought they would have dried up by now. My tears gave the streetlights a halo hue as if being viewed through waxed paper. The way the lights on the Christmas tree appeared when I squinted my eyes tight; a distant memory of something I liked to do during much more pleasant times in another life.

It was three in the morning, and the absence of other cars on the street gave me some reprieve. No one was out at this hour. God, I wished I wasn't. I looked down at my bloody hands that gripped the steering wheel of the SUV—Troy's blood.

"So much blood," I mumbled. How had I managed to grab the knife from the kitchen drawer and stick it in him? It was still a blur, his fingers choking the life out of me—he was twice my size, I couldn't breathe, I couldn't breathe.

For weeks I'd prepared to leave him, planning to go before things got too bad. I'd saved money, hid it away, but did I have enough? It didn't matter now. I'd waited too long. I'd waited, and it got far worse than I'd ever imagined.

As I clutched the collar of the tan trench coat with

my clean hand, I thought about how I should have stopped to wash my hands, should have put on some clothes. Thank God I'd left my shoes in the SUV yesterday, a habit I'd gotten into after ruining several pairs over the last year in our rain-soaked, muddy driveway. I was stark naked under my coat, but all I could think about was getting far away as quickly as possible. Running all the way upstairs to put on clothes seemed too risky. He would have killed me this time. If I hadn't stabbed him, he would have killed me. I'd taken a huge chance running to the kitchen when he'd left me beaten to a pulp on the floor of the bedroom to relieve his bladder. I barely had enough time to get downstairs and grab the knife.

I glanced in the mirror as I drove—my left eye was starting to swell and turn an ugly shade of purple mixed with black and blue. I reached up to rub at the pain on the back of my head only to find a huge bump. That bump must have happened when my head collided with the wall. The ensuing headache would surely need something more than a couple of ibuprofen. How many times did he strike me this time? I lost count after the second one. I prayed that he hadn't broken any ribs, the pain in my side was excruciating. I needed to pull over somewhere and wash, possibly ditch the SUV. That was the plan I'd had swirling around in my brain for the past three months. Dump the SUV, take a taxi to a used car lot, and buy a cheap car with the cash I'd saved. And maybe he wouldn't be able to track me.

I merged onto Interstate 5 cutting off a guy in a red Honda Civic. He swerved to the other lane and gave me the finger. It was still a couple of hours before rush hour, and I hadn't anticipated any traffic.

"Sorry, sorry," I squealed out through the closed window, and then I white-knuckled the steering wheel and forged ahead. I glanced at the gas gauge. "Crap, only half-full." After about three hours the needle teetered on empty, and I pulled off the freeway to a service station.

The sun was only beginning to light the sky, but I searched in my purse for some dark glasses anyway. I managed to hide my hands in my coat pockets and hurried to the facilities. My heart beat so fast I thought it would jump out of my chest. A twinge of relief swept over me as I discovered the bathroom was one of those one-room deals. I locked the door and washed up. Nothing came out of the hot water faucet, so I ran my bloodstained hands under freezing cold water. Once I removed the blood and splashed the chilly water on my face, I stared at myself in the mirror. Both eyes—swollen from crying—were in need of some make-up, but my left eye—black and blue, and almost swollen completely shut—was beyond help. I wasn't going to be able to do much about my eye except wear dark glasses, which somehow miraculously covered most of it.

No more tears, I ordered myself. It's over. Was he dead? I hoped he was dead. I had to have killed him. My emotions—convoluted with anger and fear—

dominated my judgment, giving me courage to go on. I'd never considered myself weak, to allow a man to have such complete and utter control over me—to beat me whenever he had the whim. How the hell had that happened?

Well, that person was gone and I didn't want to be weak anymore. I lifted my glasses, studied my eye again, and thought of my mother—she'd been weak, I remembered. The vision of my stepfather beating my mother to death invaded my mind. I was nine at the time, and sat cowering in the corner, praying he wouldn't come at me when he'd finished with her. I'd watched him slap my mom around before, and she'd always been able to recover. But that last time, he'd gone too far. I watched as my mother fell to her knees, clutching her stomach as his foot came off the ground and struck her in the face. She'd fallen backwards and her head hit the edge of the red, brick hearth of the fireplace. I covered my eyes and screamed as blood spewed out all over the bricks and the worn out, dingy cream carpet. A neighbor heard the screaming and called the police. They'd gotten there in time for me, but too late for my mother.

I'd been on my own since I was eighteen after enduring one foster home after another, never really fitting in. But at the tender age of fourteen I'd found my niche. An old discarded second-hand guitar I'd discovered in someone's trash became my savior. As long as I had a guitar in my hands nothing else mattered. After a few months of living with some friends and several temporary gigs here and there, I'd been lucky enough to find a spot with a smalltime band singing and playing lead-guitar. They called themselves The Magic Crew. They were good too, on their way to stardom, and I was right there with them until Troy Harington showed up and swept me off my feet.

It seemed as if it had all been a dream as I thought about how he'd manipulated me into believing he loved me. Handsome? Oh yeah, he was handsome with his six-foot muscle-bound frame and curly brown hair. He had dark blue eyes that could lure a fish out of the water, and lips that could talk their way in or out of any situation that might arise. Girls flocked to his side whenever he came around to listen to us play, begging him to dance with them. Like all the other girls I'd found him irresistible, and he'd chosen me over all of them. How lucky. But I soon learned it was all a subterfuge when his charm turned to violent domination.

I secretly planned and saved money over several months. A little here, a little there. I'd sneak it out of the allowance he gave me to purchase food so he wouldn't catch on. I even managed to acquire a fake ID from Weezer, a friend from my days in The Magic Crew. Weezer's real name was Wesley, but everyone called him Weezer because of his asthma, which he kept under control with his inhaler. Most times. Sometimes it got bad during certain months like springtime and fall. I'd taken him into the emergency room more than once for breathing treatments. He never seemed to mind the nickname. In fact, Weezer was the name he used when he introduced himself to people. He supplied the ID with no questions asked. I think he already knew why I wanted it, but before he would let me have it he made me promise that if I ever left town to let him know where I went. I agreed, but I knew I wouldn't tell him, at least not right away. It was better if he didn't know in case Troy ever questioned him.

I hadn't planned to leave just yet though. I would have preferred to have saved more money and had a packed suitcase ready and hidden somewhere. That last idea was a risky one, and I never got the nerve to pack one. Troy started with that same backhanded slap across my cheek—and I knew it well—but when he threw me across the room and my head smacked against the wall, the decision became a now or never deal, even with bruises and a black eye. And what was that pain in my side? Troy had been more dangerous than ever before. Killing him before he killed me seemed like my only option. Kill him and run. The words I'd said to myself right before I stabbed him. I ran, leaving everything except the coat on my back and my stash of cash.

I stepped out of the restroom and clutched my coat tightly against the bite of the wind. It was still early in the morning; clouds surrounded the sun, caressing it with cotton pillows as it began to peek from behind the mountains. I suffered the cold, reached in my purse, pulled out my cell phone and dialed a taxi service.

"Yeah, uh, can you send a cab to …" I glanced up at the sign at the small convenience store, "… the Stop N Shop on the corner of Golden and Spruce? … Okay. Fifteen minutes? Great. Thanks. I'll be waiting beside a black Explorer. … No. I don't need a tow truck. It's not my car. I'll just be standing by it. … Yeah. Thanks."

Chapter 3

Jackson

I hadn't had a chance to talk to my brother this morning considering the red scarf on his doorknob. The scarf was a don't-bother-me-I-have-company warning. I wondered who the lucky chick was this time. Or should I say "unlucky." My brother never had sex with the same woman more than twice before he'd move on, leaving a path of broken hearts in his wake. Brodie'd had some major commitment issues for the past couple of years.

The lights were on, which meant either he showed or had left the lights on last night. I stood studying the room, and heard a grunt and then the shatter of glass come from the back room behind the bar. I had just come in to take advantage of the acoustics, and to make sure Brodie showed up in time to meet the morning beer delivery. I owned the small pub but seldom worked in it. Aside from keeping track of the finances, the most I ever did was occasionally play my guitar on the small stage toward the back with the band. Every so often I'd fill in behind the bar on a busy Friday or Saturday night, but I left most of the bartending to Brodie and other employees.

"Shit," Brodie's irritated curse rang out from the room. I hurried to the stage and leaned my guitar against a chair. I'd planned to take advantage of my early morning trip to the bar to get some much needed practice in since the sound system was better here than at home. I strolled to the back room to find Brodie crouched over a toppled over case of beer. Foaming beer with shards of broken brown glass pooled around his black high tops.

"What happened?"

"That's a stupid question. What the hell do you think happened?"

"Maybe you need to spend more time at the gym and less time in the boudoir, sweet brother o' mine."

"Fuck you."

I chuckled and got a bucket for the broken bottles. "Looks like half the case is gone."

"Yeah, but I think we still got enough to get us through until the next delivery. I'll push the Hefeweizen today."

"Sounds like a plan," I agreed. I always let Brodie

make most of those decisions anyway. He ran the bar. He enjoyed it. I didn't. I helped him pick up the broken bottles and stack the good ones into the fridge.

"Thanks," he said, then stopped to stare at me. "What are you doing here, anyway?"

"I came in to check out a song I've been toying with. The sound system is better here."

He nodded. "Do me a favor, check Derrick's figures from last night, will you?" We got slammed, and we sort of closed up in a hurry."

"Because you had a …"

"A date, yeah."

"That's an exaggeration of the word."

"Whatever. Hey, man, I don't interfere with your sex life, or lack of. By the way, you need to get laid pretty soon or you're liable to spontaneously combust from sperm buildup." He laughed.

"I have my share. I just don't go blabbing about it to you."

"That's because nobody wants to hear about how tight you grip yourself when you're not hugging your guitar."

I flipped him off as I strolled out toward the stage, shaking my head and laughing to myself at our warped display of brotherly love, but Brodie had a point. It had been awhile since I had the pleasure of being with a woman, but Brodie had enough for both of us. I didn't need or want any one-nighters.

I took the guitar out of its case, wanting to play for

a while, but stood it back up against the chair again remembering the register. I cursed silently and turned back toward the bar. Work before play, I reminded myself. Brodie and I were close, and even though we teased each other, we were brothers and looked out for one another. We were all we had, and I worried about Brodie and his promiscuity sometimes.

Chapter 4

Lena

I sat on the curb, took the battery out of my cell phone, and picked up a rock while I waited for the taxi. I smashed the dinky cheap phone, shattering the plastic casing until it lost all semblance of any form of communication. Bits and pieces of pink plastic, a smashed LCD screen swirling with blue liquid, and thin wires dangling with tiny parts I didn't have a clue about lay scattered in the gutter. I gathered them all up and stood, chucking the whole mess in the bushes. I'd worry about saving the planet another time. My phone hadn't been anything fancy, but it did have GPS. Just in case I hadn't killed Troy, I didn't want him to find me—or the police, in case he

21

was dead. That would make me a murderer. I wasn't too sure how I felt about that. I locked the SUV, and threw the keys in my purse, better not to leave them anywhere near the vehicle. Not that it mattered—he had a second set. Then I reconsidered ... Why not? And dropped the keys on the ground in hopes someone would come along and steal the damn thing giving me an extra edge in my escape.

The taxi pulled into the station and stopped just inches in front of me. The driver rolled down the window and smiled, his bushy gray mustache hugged the sides of his lips in a Yosemite Sam fashion. He reminded me of a picture I'd once seen of a little girl reaching her arms up toward an older man I'd presumed to be the girl's grandfather.

"Morning, ma'am, you call for a taxi?"

"Yeah, thanks for coming so quickly." I slid into the back seat keeping my head and eyes down. The warmth of the cab felt good, and I rubbed my hands together combating the chill that seemed to linger in them from the cold bathroom water.

"No worries. I'd hate to be standing out there waiting for a taxi in the middle of the night for very long. Came as quickly as I could. Where you headed?"

I thought I'd head south into California. I didn't think this taxi driver would want to go that far, so I figured a bus or train would be my best option. "Do you know where the nearest bus stop is?"

"Well, now," he said, fingering his mustache, "You'd best go to the bus terminal. It's about twenty minutes from here." The driver's silver-white hair glistened, and his dark brown eyes twinkled, as he glanced at me in the rear-view mirror. He was friendly and full of chitchat, not requiring much interaction from me. For that, I was extremely grateful—in fact, he practically conducted the entire conversation alone. We reached the bus station, and I paid him the twenty-seven dollars showing on his meter, plus tipped him an additional five.

"Thanks. Now you just go in and ask for the South bound bus. They'll take care of you."

"Thanks," I returned, exiting the warmth of the taxicab. My fingers were still frozen, so I shoved them into my coat pockets and headed inside toward the sign that said, "Tickets."

The bus came roaring into the terminal just as I finished paying. I ran to the curb as the doors hissed open and I stepped up, dropping the ticket into the slot. Conscious of my appearance I kept my face toward the floor and walked toward the back.

The bus was almost empty except for a couple of women. A middle-aged woman whose caramel colored face gave me a thin smile as she clutched a large, grey, over-stuffed canvas bag closer to her. The bag took up the entire seat next to her. I continued down the aisle passing a young, blonde-haired woman holding the chubby hand of a small boy who sat next to her. His eyes focused on me as he squirmed out of her grasp and turned in his seat to watch me sink into the seat two rows behind him.

"Turn around, Sammy," the woman next to him scolded. He ignored her request and continued to stare at me. I gave him a small smile, and then scooted over to the seat next to the window so I could stare out at the road. I sighed. I was on my way. Resting my head against the cold glass I stared out at the old brick building of the bus terminal until it was no longer within my sight, saying goodbye to that life. To a life where every day I worried about whether or not I'd be slapped or punched in the face, tossed across the room, or kicked in the side.

I tried not to think about the possibility of the police looking for me as soon as they discovered Troy's body. I didn't know how long that would be since we never socialized much, the bruises on my face preventing such conventional activities as get-togethers, and friends were a thing of the past.

I let the ride soothe my nerves as the bus lumbered its way down the highway. Trees blurred as we skated past them. I was exhausted, and eventually the purr of the engine must have lured me to sleep. The sudden jolt of a stop and the hissing sound of the doors opening startled me awake. I glanced around, not sure how long I'd been riding. A surge of hope formed in my heart, and I got excited when I saw the two signs on the side of the road. *Millstop two miles*, the other, *Jessie's Used Cars*. Perfect, I just hoped I'd saved up enough money to buy something decent.

I gathered up my purse and rose, happy to discover

the bus was now empty. I stepped down the large steps and walked across the street to the small but clean-looking used car dealership. As I strolled onto the lot, I spotted a 2002 dark blue Subaru four-door hatchback. The bright letters painted across the windshield, ~~$5,000~~. *Just reduced to $2,000.*

"Here we go," I whispered, reminding myself to be calm. I approached a man in a grey suit standing by the open glass door to a building that housed a couple other nicer looking cars. His opened jacket revealed a blue and white-spotted tie that was tucked into his pants. "Excuse me. I'm interested in that blue Subaru out there."

The salesclerk eyed me sympathetically. "I take it you were in an accident recently," he said, smiling. "Totaled your car?"

"Yeah, the guy came out of nowhere," I said, taking advantage of the supplied excuse for the way I must have looked. It sounded like a reasonable explanation for my condition, and one I would probably use over the next several days.

After we finished all the necessary paperwork using my fake ID—Lana Martin, my mother's maiden name—for the registration, I handed over the cash, and he plopped the keys into my hand. He never questioned the fact that I paid in full, with cash, but then I suppose two thousand dollars wasn't really all that much money.

As I waited for the clerk to clean the writing off the windshield, I went into the bathroom and cut up all my credit cards—they were in Troy's name anyway—and flushed them down the toilet a few pieces at a time so I wouldn't clog the plumbing. If I was careful, I might make it through the week, giving me time to find employment somewhere in some town. I was out of Oregon now and somewhere in California. I had no idea how far into the state I actually was, though I didn't think very far. I sort of remembered seeing the "Welcome to California" sign not very long ago. When I came out of the bathroom, I stopped in front of a large display holding different brochures for things to do in Northern California. I tilted my sunglasses up a little to see what they were, and smiled when my eyes fell on the words, "State of California." I snatched the map up, and making sure my shades were back in position, held up the folded booklet and turned to the girl at the counter in the lobby. "How much?"

"Five dollars."

"I reached into my bag, pulled out a five, and laid it on the counter.

"Plus forty-one cents tax," she said with a smile.

I groped around the bottom of my purse, hoping there were a couple of quarters down there. I found two and handed her both of them. "Thanks," I said when she gave me my change. I walked out of the building and headed to my new car.

My hands shook as I steered the small hatchback out of the parking lot, still unsure of where I was heading. I wanted to get away from the dealership quickly before allowing myself to study the map. I didn't want to cause any unnecessary suspicion of someone realizing I had no idea where I was, just in case I hadn't covered my tracks well enough. I had approximately two-hundred dollars in cash left after the purchase of the car. Not much, but maybe I'd get lucky and find work fast enough.

After what felt like hours on the Interstate, I decided to make a change, and turned onto Highway 89. If Troy was still alive, or even if he wasn't, I didn't want him—or anyone—to find me, so I figured the more turns I took the better. After a while, I turned off the highway and onto a small winding road, which seemed to go on forever until I finally came to an intersection. Main Street lay before me, and I turned left, heading east. It was near nine o'clock in the morning. My side ached, and I was having difficulty breathing. I had a sick feeling my rib was badly bruised, possibly broken, and exhaustion crept into my body as I drove through a small town. It's funny how hard adrenalin pumps the blood during moments of extreme fear and stress. I smiled at the little sign posted on the right side of the street. "Welcome to Turtle Lake." The sign pictured silhouetted bodies, fishing, golfing and hunting, and a turtle, of course. It looked like it just might be the friendliest place on earth. I smiled as I passed another sign with a picture of a huge boxer turtle waving, with a bubble comment that said, "Population 573." I scanned the sides of the street searching for a place to get a cup of coffee—some place dark preferably.

Nothing in that tiny town struck me as dark and private, though. I considered turning in to an ally, pulling over to rest for a short while, maybe thirty-minutes at the most. The town struck me as one of those places one only goes to for vacation. There was a coffee shop on my right, but I didn't feel comfortable going in there. This was a very small town, and it was too bright in there. Not the type of place I wanted to venture into the way I looked. I'd never be able to hide my eye in there. I noticed a few little shops selling arts and crafts and other memorabilia, but they all appeared to be closed. While stopped at the single red light at the end of what looked like the main drag, I spotted a pub just on the other side of an empty field that actually looked open. At least the front door was open.

I parked the car and caught a glimpse of myself in the rearview mirror. I tried to smooth out my long, tangled hair, but without a brush, it was hopeless. As I got out of the car, the sparkle of the tiny speck of a diamond on my left hand caught my eye. I removed the wedding ring and tossed it in the gutter. I'd be damned if I would live the rest of my life as some poor little battered wife, and I sure as hell didn't intend to ever put that ring on again. Clutching my side, I hobbled through the door of the pub.

Chapter 5

Jackson

"We're closed." The words automatically spit out of my mouth as the shape of a body appeared in the doorway that I'd accidentally left ajar."

"Oh. Sorry. The door was open. I didn't realize." With her hand clutched to the top of a raincoat, she turned to leave.

Why was she wearing a raincoat? The sun was shining last I looked. "Wait," I caught myself saying before I considered the reasons. I didn't have any, other than the fact that she looked like she was in pain. The lighting in the room was dim. I hadn't bothered to open the blinds at the front windows yet since the pub didn't open for another couple of hours. Bar stools were still propped upside down on the bar from the floor cleaning the night before. "I guess it's okay to come in. We'll be open any minute." That was a lie, but I didn't really know what else to say. She looked so helpless I didn't have the heart to turn her away.

I swiped my hand through my thick black hair thinking I should have pulled it back into a ponytail. It hung down the back of my neck and onto my shoulders. It was the longest it had ever been, and it irritated me when I did any physical work like the mundane task of balancing out a register—usually my younger brother's job—or mixing cocktails. Instead of telling her the pub wasn't open for business yet, I decided to let her come in. There was something not right with her; the way she walked, slowly and carefully, as if she were injured. I pulled a stool down from the bar and placed it on the floor gesturing for her to sit, and walked behind the bar. She clutched her coat closed as she hesitated, but then slowly walked to the stool. Her hands shook as she placed her bag down on the bar, and I decided it might be interesting to play bartender for a while.

"What can I get you?" I placed a napkin down in front of her.

"Coffee, please." She kept her head down, holding on to her dark glasses as if she could hide the bruise that protruded from under them.

I took a bottle of Jameson's down from the shelf, poured some into a shot-glass, and set it in front of her.

"I said *coffee*." Her voice was soft and trembled as

she spoke, and she looked around the place as if making sure no one else was there that she knew.

"Yeah, I know." I kept my voice soft, hoping she realized I meant no harm. "But you look like you could use this." I stood with the bottle still in my hand.

She glanced back at the open door. "I don't drink. I mean, at least not at nine in the morning."

"Well, I think you should make an exception in this case. Hell, if it makes you feel better, I'll have one too." I poured another, picked it up, and waited for her to pick hers up and join me.

"I don't think …" The words came out slowly, and she paused and looked at me. "Do I really look that bad?"

I nodded.

"Well, okay," her voice timid, she raised the glass, and I clinked mine against hers.

"Bottoms up." We emptied the glasses, and I poured her a cup of coffee. I decided to be bold and go all out. "So, where'd you get the shiner?"

"I was hoping it would be dark enough in here that it wouldn't be noticed," she said, pulling off the glasses and glanced back again at the door.

"Ouch," I couldn't help the cringe at the sight of the black eye. "Let me get some ice for that," I said, as I strolled to the front door and shut it, turning the lock. Her shoulders relaxed a bit.

"Thanks, but not necessary, I'm sure it'll be fine."

I didn't acknowledge her objection. Instead, I filled

a plastic bag with ice, wrapped it in a towel, and handed it to her. "Hold it on there for a good fifteen minutes. It'll help the swelling go down."

As I studied her, waiting for her to answer how she scored the shiner, I decided that even with the black eye she was a damn attractive girl. Her reddish brown hair, lying loose around her face—most likely to help hide her eye—would be as smooth as silk once it met a brush again. She was thin, maybe too thin. She was running from something, or someone. No one, especially a beautiful young woman, comes walking into my bar—well any bar, for that matter—at nine o'clock in the morning with a shiner double the size of a silver dollar, clutching her coat closed while hobbling over to a seat. I wondered just what was under her coat, perhaps a nightgown, sweats—or nothing.

When she hadn't answered my question, I went for a different approach.

"So, how does the other guy look?"

"Huh? Oh, yeah ... ah, the other guy ... not so good." She shook her head slowly and stared straight ahead, lost in her own thoughts.

"Lover's spat?"

She raised her hand to her face. Her cheeks flushed a little pink. "Um ... no." She was silent for a few seconds then piped up as if she'd just remembered something. "There was no other guy. I was in a car accident this morning."

I figured she was lying, particularly when I caught sight of the large handprint on her wrist protruding

32

from the sleeve of her coat.

"I don't mean to sound nosey, but have you seen a doctor yet? You could have some serious injuries, you know. The way you walked over here it looks as if you may have a broken rib—or at least cracked—maybe two."

"I'll be all right." She sipped the coffee as she held the ice pack up to her eye and sat in silence. She took her coffee black. I appreciated that. I'd never understood how someone could ruin a great cup of coffee with cream and sugar. She looked around the pub. Her gaze settled on the stage.

"You have live music here?" she asked.

"Yeah, we do. A couple nights a week, sometimes more. Mostly on Friday and Saturday nights—just some local boys and myself occasionally. It helps bring in the tourists."

She smiled and sipped her coffee again, and when she set the cup down, I topped it off.

"Thanks, um ... Where's the restroom?"

I pointed behind her. "Over there, just past the stage."

She walked slowly across the room. I'd considered offering her a hand, but decided to hold back. She didn't seem open to accepting any help, but underneath that tough exterior, I detected a lot of fear. My interest piqued as she stopped briefly to look at my guitar on the stage as she passed by.

Chapter 6
Lena

I hadn't been expecting the gallantry. I intended to come in, sit alone, and have a cup of coffee; no questions asked. That guy seemed nice and harmless though. Under different circumstances, I would have been attracted to him. He had a kind, handsome face. But then Troy had a kind face too, at one time. The man in this bar seemed to possess something Troy didn't though. Compassion. It showed in his soft green eyes. And really, how could you not want to trust someone wearing a dark purple T-shirt that said "When words fail, music speaks." The T-shirt was fitted to his torso, and revealed part of a tattoo on his well-sculpted upper arm, the only part of which I could make out was a series of music notes trailing down.

It was probably not a good idea to trust anyone right now, but it had been such a long time since a man was nice to me. Troy hadn't allowed me to socialize after we'd gotten married. He said if he caught me talking to any of my friends he'd punish me. I knew firsthand what those punishments were like. Two weeks after we eloped he showed me how things would be. How he could punish me. It didn't take long for that nice, lovable, charm to turn nasty. I tried my best to please him, but I was never good enough. There was never any warning of what might set him off. By the end of our first month of marriage I realized I'd made the biggest mistake of my life, and I feared he might kill me the way that monster had killed my mother.

Standing before the mirror I tried to smooth down my hair again, but it was no use. "God, I do look pathetic. That bartender must think I'm a case."

I rinsed my hands under the warm water. Closing my eyes as the cold tingling in my fingers subsided. As I dried my hands, I caught sight of a little bit of blood under my short fingernails. I always kept them short because of the guitar, even though it had been a while since they even touched any strings. After seeing the beautiful wooden instrument on the stage they suddenly itched to play again. I wished I still had mine. Another thing Troy had gotten rid of. He said I didn't need any reminders of that wild life, said I was better off now—

secure with him—he would give me all I would ever need. I sighed, leaving the bathroom with an overwhelming need to play that guitar.

Chapter 7

Jackson

$\mathcal{I}$ watched as she walked out of the bathroom and stopped again at the front of the stage. This time, she stepped up and picked up my most prized possession—my custom Fender Dreadnaught guitar—and my heart leaped in my chest. I started to object, but paused. The way she picked it up, stroking her fingers gently over the golden base, told me it wasn't the first time she'd held a guitar in her hands. What would it hurt? She sat down on the chair with her back facing me and began strumming a few chords. She played a soft ballad, and I was impressed.

Brodie appeared by my side, a towel draped over

his shoulder. He stood an inch taller than my six-feet-two-inches with the same green eyes, the same strong jaw line, and black hair. But Brodie's hair had an auburn hue to it, which turned redder in the summer, and he wore it shorter.

"Heard the tune," Brodie said in a low whisper. "Thought you'd gone soft on us. Who's the chick?"

"Don't know yet."

"Is that your Dreadnought she's playing?"

"Yeah."

"You're letting *her* play it, and you don't even know who she is? Sheeeeit ... if I even blink at that guitar of yours you have a hissy fit and threaten to kick my ass."

"You need to stick to your bass. Now, shut up or I will kick your ass."

Brodie chuckled. "You haven't been able to kick my ass since fourth grade."

I tilted my head toward Brodie's and whispered, "She has a shiner double the size of a silver-dollar, and she keeps clutching at her side. It looks like someone roughed her up pretty badly."

"Whoever did that to her might come looking for her, you know. They might want to finish what they started."

I frowned. "I'll handle her. You should go back to whatever it was you were doing. She seems a bit skittish, if you know what I mean. Too many faces may spook her."

"My brother, the savior ... do I need to caution

you?"

"Too late, I already gave her ice for her eye. I'm involved now." I hardly knew her, but somehow my need to help her overwhelmed me. I believed in fate. It had to be fate that brought her into my bar on a morning that I just happened to be there.

"Is this going to be like the fawn or the bird?"

It was a well-known fact—sometimes even a joke—around town, that I'd made a habit of saving injured animals. I had to admit, I'd always been a sucker for the wounded. Even as a kid I was always rescuing injured animals. When I was eleven, I rescued a fawn tangled in barbed wire. The fawn had an injured leg. I nursed it back to health and wanted to keep it— begged to keep it—but my dad said I had to let it go once it regained its strength. I cried over that fawn the day my dad took it back into the wild. I hadn't cried since, not even when the old man walked out on us, and our mother, two years later.

The hawk rescue, on the other hand, was a little bit different. It simply flew away once its wing had healed. I had been older by then, and knew it would happen, just as it had with some of the other animals I'd saved.

"Probably more like the fawn," I admitted. It was beautiful and wounded too.

"Shit. Well, don't come crying on my shoulder. I know, I know, there's nothing I can say or do to change your mind." Brodie shook his head. "At any rate, she sounds great. Looks great from this angle too. I wonder if she can sing."

"Hmmm." I rubbed my chin. Brodie was right. From this view of the side of her face you couldn't see the black eye, and she was beautiful. The idea that anyone could assault such a lovely creature sickened me. It appalled me to think about some scum of the earth beating her—major scum of the earth. My brother was also right about the possibility of someone looking for her, especially the way she kept looking at the door.

When she finished playing the tune she set the guitar down with care—gently resting it in the exact position I had placed it in earlier. She knew how to handle a guitar. That alone told me she was worth the risk. She turned and smiled when she saw me watching. I'm sure I had a silly grin on my face.

"I'm sorry, I should have asked first. I hope that was okay. Playing always seems to relax me, and when I saw it there I just couldn't help myself."

And I couldn't help myself. "No, that was lovely," I said. *She* was lovely.

She returned to her seat and carefully sat down. I dumped out her cup and filled it back up with hot coffee. I noticed her coat opened a bit at the top, revealing a bruise at her collarbone. She saw where I was looking, and tugged the coat shut. Then she picked up the cup and sipped. The way she positioned herself on the stool made me think her side was aching more now.

"I don't usually let anyone touch my baby, especially when I don't even know her name. I'm

Jackson Beaumont, by the way." I held out my hand to her, and she placed her small soft one in mine.

"Le ... um, Lana. Nice to meet you."

"The pleasure's mine, ah, Le … um, Lana."

She giggled a little. "Just Lana."

"Okay, just Lana, then."

She nodded.

"You've got some talent, Lana."

"Thanks. I played all through high school, and actually played in a band later. We had a few gigs in some minor clubs back in Medford until ...." She trailed off, lowered her eyes, and became silent. I figured she wasn't willing to reveal too much information, not even her real name.

"You're welcome to jam with us any night, or are you just passing through?" I poured myself a cup of coffee. I wasn't accustomed to having a swig of whiskey in the morning, and I decided that I had a busy day ahead and needed a clear mind.

"No, I haven't really given it much thought, but yeah, I'm just passing through ... I think." Then she grabbed at her side and cringed with discomfort.

"Look, um ... Lana, I can tell you're in pain, and I can also tell you're scared. No one here will hurt you. You know … I have a friend, Doc. He could take a look at your injuries if you want."

"No. No doctors. I can't."

"It's okay. Doc's not really a doctor. We just call him Doc. His real name is Jon Doctrill. We've called him Doc since we were kids. He's a little older than me, and he had a short stint in the Army—medical unit—after he'd gone through pre med. After his term in Iraq he decided to shine on the medical career. Said he'd seen enough blood for one lifetime. Now he just sort of hangs out around here and plays in the band when he's not risking his life for the fire department. I'm sure he'd be happy to take a look, make sure nothing's broken."

"No. I can't ask you to do that, really. I'll be fine. Besides, I really should be going."

"Yeah ... I know," I said softly and leaned closer to her, my forearm resting on the bar. I didn't want her to leave. "But it's no trouble. Really. He's due in here any minute anyway, and he owes me," I lied. Jon wasn't expected to come in, but he did owe me.

"How about I give him a call, get him here a bit sooner. Let him check out your eye and your side. You can barely move. Then, if you want, you can be on your way. No questions asked. If nothing else, at least he can give you some pain meds. He seems to have a never ending supply."

"No, really, I can't. You're kind, but no thanks."

She started to get up to leave, and I laid my hand on hers, and looked into her eyes. "Please, Lana. Let me help you."

She paused and sat back down. "I don't know. I could use a few pain meds I guess. Are you sure he won't mind?"

"I promise, and you won't even have to pay him."

"Are you always in the habit of rescuing young

women?"

"Yeah, I'm a real boy scout. Yesterday I helped poor old Mrs. Feeney across the street, and if you stick around, I'll show you how to build a fire from a few twigs and a rock."

She chuckled and grabbed at her side.

"I really did help Mrs. Feeney. Just not across the street. It was more like rescuing her cat from a tree branch that was just out of her reach. But as far as the fire goes, we'll have to use matches." That made her laugh out loud, which in turn caused her to clutch at her side and moan. Man, I was doing nothing but causing this poor girl more pain.

As I dialed Doc's number, I glanced over at Lana, glad for once that the portable phone had been left at the far end of the bar, which gave me an excuse to walk away to talk.

"Hey, Doc. Glad you're in."

"What's up Jack? I was just on my way down there."

"Guess I didn't lie after all."

"Huh?"

"Never mind. Listen. Bring your medical bag with you. There's a girl here I want you to check out."

"A girl? What, you want me to check to make sure she's a safe lay? Come on Jack, I don't give physicals. Tell her to go see a doctor."

I glanced back at Lana and whispered, "She's in pretty bad shape, Doc. I think she may have a bruised rib, maybe cracked. She said she was in a car accident, but she's scared, and doesn't want any doctors. She won't say why, but … I think she was beaten up, maybe even raped."

Chapter 8

Lena

I glanced up to see the frame of a towering man stroll into the bar, the top of his head just missing the door lintel. His stride matched his length, and he eyed me suspiciously as he passed by me. A red-checkered patch at the base of one of the pockets on his rear end caught my eye. A stray curl fell over his left eye, somehow escaping the light brown ponytail, the end licking across the center of his back. Black medical looking bag in tow, I assumed this was Doc. He walked—no, strutted—over to Jackson. Definitely not your average looking soldier boy. To me, he looked as though nature had placed him in the wrong era, thirty years out of his time.

"Hey Doc, this is Lana. Lana, Jon Doctrill." I wondered if it was safe to let him examine me. I wanted to run out of there. I started to stand, winced at the pain, and clutched my side. Jackson grabbed my arm to steady me, and helped me to sit back down. "Whoa. Take it easy."

"Seems to be getting worse," I admitted. My voice sounded weak, even to me.

"Maybe I can help," Doc said.

I gave him a wary look, still not quite sure how much I could trust him, even trust Jackson for that matter.

Doc took a step toward me, and I cowered back a step. "What harm could it do?" Doc tilted his head and shrugged his shoulders.

"He's right, what harm could it do?" Jackson said.

"Lana." Doc held out his hand and smiled a don't-worry-I'll-take-care-of-you smile. His kind eyes put me a little more at ease.

"Let's go back to the office for privacy, just in case someone else comes in."

My muscles must have started to tighten up because walking now was much more difficult than it had been just a short while ago. Leaning on Jackson for support, I hobbled along to a small room in the back of the bar.

"Here, sit down Lana." Jackson gestured toward a small brown leather sofa along the wall before turning to leave.

"Wait, please stay," I begged, still unsure of what I

was getting myself into. I somehow felt a little safer with Jackson there.

"I'll need you to take off your coat so I can listen to your lungs and check your ribs."

Remembering I didn't have anything on underneath my coat, I only unbuttoned the top three buttons. My hands trembled with each small movement.

"Um ... I'll need more than that," he said.

"I uh ... sort of left in a hurry, and didn't really have time to put much on."

"Sorry, here. You can cover up with this." Doc picked up a small wool blanket from the back of the sofa and handed it to me. I didn't like the idea of baring my flesh to this stranger, but I knew I was hurt, and I didn't want to go to the emergency room for treatment. Hospitals and urgent care centers asked too many questions, and quite honestly, I wasn't that great of a liar. At this point, I figured Doc was my only solution. I was grateful when Jackson turned his back. Doc frowned as he gazed at the myriad of bruises on my sides. "Okay, just breathe as deep as you can," he said, holding his stethoscope against my back.

I winced as each breath caused a stabbing pain through my midsection.

"Now lie back, I'm going to check your ribs to make sure you're not showing any signs of internal problems. It may hurt a bit."

He was gentle with his touch as he examined my rib cage, but I cringed anyway when his fingers met my skin. I didn't think I'd ever be able to allow another man to touch me in any way after Troy, and I had to remind myself that Doc was a doctor, almost. Deep down I knew most men were not like Troy.

"Sorry, I know that must hurt like a mother fucker."

"Jeez Doc, watch your language will you?" Jackson grumbled from the door.

"Sorry, I mean hurt like a son of a bitch. Ah shit, sorry."

In spite of the pain and the embarrassment of the situation, I smiled at Doc's flustering.

"You can sit up now," he said, holding out a hand for me. I grabbed it, and as I sat up and pulled the blanket around me, Jackson turned back around.

Jackson waited patiently across the room as Doc checked the bump on my head and examined my eye, asking me to follow his finger as he checked my peripheral vision, which I'm pretty sure was fine.

Doc straightened. "I'm sorry … I have to ask this, but is there any semen residue we need to be concerned with? You know, in case you want to press charges?"

"Really, Doc? She said she was in a car accident," Jackson said.

Doc shot Jackson an apologetic look. "Sorry, it's just the way these bruises are shaped, I just assumed ... sorry, I had to ask."

"I'm sure Lana knows the law concerning rape, Doc. Of course they would need a sample of the semen to prosecute. Right Lana?"

I understood what Jackson was getting at. He was stating the law for my benefit. He didn't believe my accident story any more than Doc did. Could he really think I was that ignorant? Of course he could, he didn't know me.

I smiled at Jackson, and appreciated the way he had stayed with his back to us while Doc examined me. "It's okay. No, there isn't," I said, remembering how Troy had lost his erection in the middle of what he deemed lovemaking. At least that was something I didn't need to lie about.

"How long ago did this happen?" Doc asked.

"Um …" I didn't know what to say. I hadn't planned on being questioned by anyone. I'd planned on hiding out somewhere quiet until my wounds healed, but now that I realized how badly I looked, I knew that the little bit of money I had would never make it until then. "Early this morning ... I was in a friend's car. We pulled out of the driveway and bam, a truck smacked right into my side of the back of our SUV. We were on our way to visit friends. My friend decided to stay home and get their car fixed so I left on my own. I've been driving for about six hours since, I think." Disbelief settled over both of their faces, and they glanced at each other, but I continued with my ruse.

Doc didn't mention anything else about my condition or the fact that I was completely naked under my coat.

"Well, an X-ray would be helpful, but rib fractures

don't always show up on X-ray. You don't seem to be having too much difficulty breathing, which would indicate that there's not too much damage. I'd say your ribs are most likely just badly bruised, but not too bad. You should avoid taking too many deep breaths, as those will only aggravate your injuries more. You'll want to keep ice on that eye, and some on your head. Jackson can help you to do that." He glanced at Jackson and he nodded. "I have something for the pain, but you shouldn't drive while taking it. Actually, you shouldn't travel anywhere for a while. A little bed rest and you'll be good as new."

I wasn't sure what to do at that point. I didn't have any place to go. "Thanks," I said, and I dropped my head in my hands to think.

Jackson cleared his throat and said, "We'll be out here. Come out when you're ready." He nodded to Doc and tilted his head toward the door as they stepped out.

Chapter 9
Jackson

Doc and I walked to the bar, and Doc wiped his brow frowning at me. "She said she'd been driving for about six hours, Jack, which would indicate that her injuries aren't as bad as they look. Sometimes adrenalin kicks in and takes over and you don't realize how much pain you're actually in. I've seen it before. She ought to be careful and take it easy for a while. That bump on the back of her head is nasty—so for the next twenty-four hours, no sleeping longer than a couple of hours at a time. You know the drill."

"Yeah, I do." I nodded, remembering the time Brodie and I went snowboarding last winter. Brodie tried to be a little too macho, and went way too fast on a jump. He landed on his head, and for several seconds he couldn't even feel his legs. The ski patrol had to come and tow him down the mountain. It had to have been the scariest moment in my life.

Doc placed his hand on my shoulder. "Jackson, what the fuck are you getting yourself into? You know she's lying, you know someone beat the crap out of her. Most likely a boyfriend or husband, and you know he's gonna come looking for her. She should be in a shelter for battered women where she can get the proper care and attention she needs, but shit, considering you called me, I guess that would be out of the question. Did you know she doesn't even have any clothes on under that coat?"

I crossed my arms over my chest, and nodded thoughtfully. "Yeah, I noticed that, and yes, a shelter would be a great place for her, but I know there has to be a good reason she didn't go to one. A reason she hasn't divulged yet. She's scared. I know I'm a sucker for the wounded, but I want to help."

"Look, Jack, I know you only have the best intentions, but I have a weird feeling about this. It could have been a rape. A lot of women lie about that and won't go to the police, but if it wasn't, then some mean son-of-a-bitch husband did this to her, and getting mixed up in domestic affairs with strangers is bad news. You don't know what kind of maniac did this."

"She doesn't seem old enough to have a husband," I said thoughtfully, thinking about Jonah White and

Emily Baker who'd gotten married right out of high school and reconsidered. "I'll find out." I knew I could. I just needed some time—or rather, she needed time to trust me. I wanted to make sure she felt safe, and didn't want her to think I'd betray her trust. I wanted her to know that I'd keep my word and wouldn't call the authorities. I also knew that in rape cases, if this was a rape case, Doc was right. Some women would go the police after a rape, but there were many who wouldn't. But something told me this wasn't some random attack. She was more frightened than distressed. I felt sure she was running from someone. "It would be best if you kept this to yourself, okay?"

Doc shook his head but said, "Yeah, sure."

As he turned to leave I placed my hand on his back. "Doc, thanks. I'll see you later. Come in early. I'll buy you a beer before you go on tonight." I patted Doc on the shoulder as we walked toward the door. I wanted to make sure to lock it after he left.

"Yeah? Fucking A, you can buy me a few. How's that?"

"Deal."

After shutting the door and locking it, I turned to see Brodie standing on the other side of the bar drying a beer glass with a smirk on his face, shaking his head. I pointed a finger at him about to tell him to wipe the smirk off his face and mind his own business when Lana walked out of the office, tugging her coat tightly together.

She didn't make an excuse to bolt as I thought she might. Instead, she smiled with chagrin and went to sit back at the bar.

"Oh, Lana, this is my brother Brodie."

"Hello," Brodie said still wiping the same glass he'd been drying for the past couple of minutes.

"Hello."

I wanted Brodie to leave, so I gestured my head toward the back, but he ignored me. "Don't you have some beer to put away back there?"

"Oh," he said, feigning stupidity, or maybe it was real. "Yeah. Ah ... nice to meet you, Lana."

I poured her more coffee after dumping the cold one out, again.

"Um ... Jackson."

"Yeah?"

Her eyes connected with mine. "Actually, it's Lena," she said, finally admitting to lying about her name. "And thanks. Sorry I lied about my name." Progress, I thought and smiled, keeping my eyes on hers. God, beneath the black and blue and the swelling, she had gorgeous eyes.

"You're welcome, Lena. According to Doc, you need rest and time to recuperate." I was glad she decided to trust me enough to tell me her real name—at least her first name.

"I got that. Only problem is I don't know where that should be. Are there any inexpensive hotels around here?"

"No. No inexpensive ones, but today's your lucky

day. Well, lucky from here on out."

"How's that?" she asked, sipping the hot coffee.

"Well, lucky you walked in to *my* bar, and lucky that just last week the tenant who rented the cottage above my garage moved out, and I haven't re-rented it yet. You can stay there while you heal if you'd like. It's furnished."

She fell silent for a moment then asked, "How much?"

"No charge."

"No. I couldn't do that."

"Yes you can. Please, trust me."

She sighed and shook her head. "Trusting you isn't the issue. I want to, but I'm not a charity case. I would like to pay you."

"We can discuss that later. For now, you need to be somewhere safe, and my cottage is perfect."

"Are you sure?"

"I insist."

"I could pay you some now. I don't have much money, but ..."

"Tell you what, when your eye heals, and you feel well enough, you can provide me the pleasure of hearing you play some more on my guitar. Maybe join in some night here at the bar. How's that sound?"

"I don't know why you're being so nice to me, nor do I know if ... well, my gut tells me I should trust you. But then, I don't know. I haven't done so great in the trusting-men-department lately, so forgive me if I sound a bit skeptical here, but why do you care?"

"Let's just say I like the way you played my Dreadnought."

Brodie came out from the back room carrying a case of beer. "Don't you think we should open the door now? It's getting close to eleven-thirty."

He set the case down and started stocking the fridge.

I looked at Lena as she grabbed her coat closed tighter. "Give us a minute and we'll be out of here. I'm going to show Lena the cottage and get her settled in."

"The cottage?" Brodie frowned then shook his head as he lined the small refrigerator with the rest of the beer, emptying the case. We were close for brothers, not only in age—Brodie being only eleven months younger—but close friends as well.

"Okay, Jackie," he said with a bit of a shrill to his voice, sending a shiver down my back. He knew it would irritate me—always had, ever since we were kids when Jenny Casings wrote Jackie and Jenny all over the girls' bathroom in elementary school. From then on, it was a continuous tease of Jackie and Jenny, J and J, Jackie loves Jenny. It was a small town, and I had to grow up hearing Jackie and Jenny most of my life. It got worse in eighth grade when I had actually given in, and agreed to go with Jenny Casings to the Sadie Hawkins dance. She had a crush on me since second grade, and never quite got over me until Brad Sims came along in high school and swept her off her feet. Thank God. Then she became Mrs. Brad Sims, and I couldn't have been more pleased. It wasn't that Jenny was bad looking or anything; she just talked incessantly, which annoyed the hell out of me.

Although I knew Lena could drive—she'd driven all morning—I didn't think she should anymore in her condition. So, we left her car on the street by the bar. She didn't strike me as the type of woman to put up with abuse, but perhaps that's why she was running. If so, I had to give her credit.

The guest cottage stood behind the main house on a huge lot my uncle had owned. I pulled my car to the back and stopped in front of the garage door. In order to get to the cottage we'd need to walk up a steep set of stairs beside the garage, and I wasn't entirely sure Lena would be able to make the climb. I went to offer her a hand up the stairs as she quailed, and I wondered if she cowered out of fear or habit. I held on to her anyway, determined to win her trust, and helped her up the long flight of stairs that led to the front door. To the left of the landing at the top of the stairs our newly installed wood deck balcony graced the front and protruded out above the garage doors. "It's not much, but it should meet your needs for a few days or however long you need it."

Lena almost jumped out of her skin at the sound of the deep, rough bark that came from half way up the stairs as my massive hound dog, complete with drooping ears and loose wrinkled skin, came trudging up with drool dripping from his jowls.

"That'd be Rufus. He'll be your best friend if you rub behind his ears. Otherwise, he'll just lie beside your feet. Though if you're not careful, he just might lie on top of them, and believe me, he can be quite heavy."

"Hi there, Rufus." Lena let go of her coat, crouched down to the dog and rubbed the loose wrinkled skin around his ears as I opened the door to the cottage. "He's great, how old is he?" she asked, letting the dog slobber all over her.

"Ah, he's about five now. He seems to like you, but if you're not careful, you're going to need a bath after he finishes drooling all over you."

"Yeah, well, I need a bath anyway, huh Rufus," she said with a low voice, pouting her lips as she spoke close to the dog's head, making my fondness for her grow immensely.

Her coat hung off her shoulder revealing soft looking white skin, and surprise came over me as I realized I was staring. I thought maybe I should reach down and tug it up before Rufus nuzzled it down any further, but then decided to let it go. I had to remind myself to be careful, she was in no shape for what was going through my mind. "He's a great tracker, but voracious. He eats about ten pounds of dog food a week."

Lena stood up and pulled her coat closed as she walked through the door I held open. "Thanks." She stepped in, glanced around. "This is perfect."

"It's just a one-room deal, furnished with a small daybed, a couple of end tables, and an old television. There's a small kitchen with your basic ceramic sink, refrigerator, and small stove. The bathroom has a shower and a small tub that you can soak in ... if you want." I cleared my throat as I forced that picture out of my head. I really needed to get a handle on where my mind was going. This girl was injured, in more ways than one.

"Um ... listen, I have some clothes you could put on. Nothing fancy, and I'm sure they'll be three sizes too big for you, but at least you won't have to wear your coat all the time. I'll go get them. I live in the house down there." I pointed to the large three story stone house that sat on the other side of the driveway in front of our massive backyard—close to two acres— spanning down to the three-foot wide creek that flowed most of the year.

Lena glanced out the window. "You mean that park down there is part of your backyard? I guess with a dog like Rufus you would need a backyard that size."

"Yeah. You sit. Relax. I'll be right back. Rufus stay."

It wasn't like me to eavesdrop, and I had full intentions of walking straight down those steps, but when I closed the door I heard her speaking to Rufus, and the sound of her sweet fragile voice had me frozen in my steps.

"Ahhh, Rufus. I'm so scared. What's going to

happen to me? If they find Troy's body they'll surely put me in jail. I know he would have killed me this time. I don't think they'll believe me. Do you believe me Rufus?"

Who was Troy? And did she kill him? If so, it must have been self-defense. But then why was she running?

I pictured her hands on the dogs face, looking at him square in the eye, and Rufus licking her chin. I knew my dog, knew he'd nuzzle up against her leg with an assiduous look to his deep-set eyes as if he understood every word she said.

"You're a good dog, aren't you, Rufus, boy. Yeah, you like that don't cha?"

Realizing I stood frozen and riveted over each and every one of her words, I forced myself down the steps to retrieve the promised, but almost forgotten, clothes. After rummaging through my drawers searching for those small grey sweat pants I had back in high school, I finally found them in a corner on the floor of my closet. When and how they got there, I had no clue. Less than ten minutes later I raced back up the stairs, juggling a couple of long sleeve thermal shirts and the grey sweat pants in my arms. I didn't just walk right in though. I knocked before opening the door about an inch, and asked if it was okay to come in.

"Yeah sure, of course."

"Here's a pair of sweat pants that are small on me and might fit better than my others, and a couple of shirts.

"Thanks."

Beautifully Wounded

"I'll see what I might be able to come up with from one of Brodie's girlfriends, but in the meantime, these should work." I handed her the clothes as our furry grey and white cat slinked her way past me and rubbed up against Lena.

"That's Rosie, she'll rub the heck out of your legs if you don't pick her up and pet her for a few minutes, but you should go ahead and change. I'll be back in a few and get you set up with some clean bedding."

She picked up the cat, stroked her head, and smiled as she looked up at me with a bemused expression. "*One* of his girlfriends?"

"Yeah, that's Brodie. Anyway, you can go ahead and change if you want. I'll be back up in a few."

"Jackson ... if it's okay, I think I'd like to bathe first. I um ..."

"Oh yeah." How inconsiderate of me. Anyone in their right mind would want to shower after what she'd been through. "Of course. Sorry. I wasn't thinking. Let me just make sure that there's some soap in there. I'll run down and get you some towels and stuff."

Chapter 10

Lena

I sat on the daybed looking around, noting there were no pictures on the walls, and very little furniture, and that the kitchen counters were completely bare. Then I remembered he'd said it was a rental. I patted the dog some more and stroked the cat before taking the clothes into the bathroom. I set them on top of the counter and ran the water in the tub, letting it run over my fingers as it filled. I debated as to whether I should wait for him to come back up with towels before plunging in, but the water looked so inviting, and I felt so filthy and grungy. I couldn't wait to get the smell of Troy off me. I shrugged out of my coat, let it fall to the floor, and stepped into the warm, soothing water. Resting my head against the back of the tub, I closed my eyes, and for the first time in a year I relaxed, almost. I thought … maybe I was even safe. But was I?

I didn't want to run for the rest of my life. If I had managed to kill Troy, how long would it take the police to find me? If I didn't kill him, how long would it take him to find me? I wasn't sure which situation was better, but settled on the first one. I'd rather go to prison than be subjected to Troy's abuse again. How did other women deal with it? I'd asked myself that question too many times.

Yes, I knew there were shelters, but as Troy reminded me many times, he'd find me if I ever tried to run, and I knew a shelter or safe house for women would be the first place he would look. I'd read hundreds of stories about abused women. I didn't think I was anything like them. I was stronger than them— stronger than my mother. Or so I'd thought. Of course, I'd never brought any of those books home. It was better to just read those types of books while at the library, never checking one out. Troy knew everything I did. It wouldn't have surprised me if he kept tabs on everything I borrowed from the library. I was lucky he would even let me go there every few weeks.

Chapter 11

Jackson

When I came back up with the towels, shampoo, and some clean sheets for the bed, I realized I'd left the front door open a bit. I knocked, but she didn't answer, so I just walked in this time figuring she knew I was coming. The water was running in the bathroom, and the door left ajar with Rufus edged in between it and the door jam. I froze when I saw her soaking in the tub. Suddenly I felt like I was back in high school as a wave of embarrassment swept over me, and I quickly turned away.

"Ah ... Lena?"

The sound of my voice must have startled her. The

water sloshed loudly, and she groaned with pain. "Ouch! I didn't hear you come in."

"Sorry, are you okay? I didn't mean to startle you. I'll just leave these towels here on this stool. I brought up some shampoo, and found some conditioner." I set the towels and plastic bottles down on a chair just inside the door to the bathroom, and turned to walk away. I stopped before leaving, and over my shoulder I said, "Oh, by the way, you might not want to stay in there too long, especially if the water is hot, the hot water isn't good for the swelling."

"Thanks, you're probably right. It just looked so inviting, but now that I'm in here, I'm not sure I can get up."

"Do you need help?" I asked, keeping my back toward her, but sounding a little too eager.

"No ... um ... yes ... I think I might, but ..."

"Don't worry, I won't look." I picked up a towel, opened it, and holding it sideways, I walked up to the side of the tub. Keeping my eyes averted, I reached in and wrapped the towel around her while helping her up.

Our eyes met. I kept mine on hers, not wanting her to think I wanted a glimpse of her body. Her one good eye, blue as the deepest part of the ocean, and the other a swollen slit of puffy black and blue, gazed into mine for a few seconds before she glanced down and placed one hand on the towel and the other up to her face in a poor attempt to hide her eye.

"Thank you. God, I must look horrible."

"You'll heal." Yeah, she did look awful. Like someone beat the crap out of her, awful. I wanted to trail my finger down the side of her cheek, wishing I could stroke away the pain. Almost as if something or someone took possession of my hand, the tips of my fingers were at the side of her face, ready to find out just how soft her skin might be. But when her mouth opened as though the gesture shocked her, I dropped my hand and stepped away. I wanted to touch her. I wanted very much to take away her pain, not only the bruises, but the mental anguish I knew she must carry inside, and the thought worried me. Just how long could I stand not touching her?

"Listen, Jackson, this is really great, what you're doing for me." Her words brought me out of all those visions I had no business thinking about. "I don't know how I'll ever repay you."

"Don't worry about it right now." I turned to walk out of the bathroom, but stopped and turned back. "If you want to shower and wash your hair, the shower controls are backwards, something I've been meaning to fix but haven't gotten around to yet."

"Okay, thanks."

I had to force myself to turn back around and walk away. Coaxing Rufus out of the way, I shut the bathroom door, and went back down to the main house. Black eye and all she was lovely, but she wasn't in any shape—emotionally or physically—for me to be thinking about her in that way. Hell, the way I saw it, she probably never would be. I swore that if this Troy character was still, alive and I ever met up with the coldblooded bastard, I'd need to have someone restrain me because I knew I'd want to kill him.

Down in my own kitchen I decided to make some eggs and toast. Considering that Lena walked into the bar around nine, and it was nearly noon now, she must be hungry. I brewed some fresh coffee and put some butter in a pan when the phone rang.

"Hello?"

"Jackson, are you coming back? You left your guitar here on the stage," Brodie said.

"Shit, um ... could you put it in the office? I don't know when I'll get back there."

"Yeah, sure. Also, where did you put the daily sheet with the liquor count on it?"

"Look in the register," I barked. Brodie knew that's where I always put it. Out of frustration, I took a couple of steps toward the doorway.

"I did, it's not there, and one of the keg spouts is jammed."

God, I hated when Brodie acted like an imbecile.

"Open your bloody eyes Brodie, and look harder. I don't have time for this. I've got things happening here."

"Yeah? Well while you're off playing hero I've got a business to run."

"My business."

"Yeah *your* business, and I'm running it by myself. So cut me some slack will you? Okay, found it, you stuck it under the twenties. By the way, how's your fawn?" There was a note of actual concern in his question.

"Mending."

I turned to the sizzling sound followed by the smell of burning butter coming from the stove. "Shit, I need to go. Talk to you later."

Chapter 12
Lena

I pulled on the over-sized sweatpants and thermal shirt. It felt good to be clean, to get the smell of Troy off me. Jackson was thoughtful enough to bring a brush up with him when he brought up the shampoo and towels. Standing in front of the mirror I brushed the tangles out of my wet hair, and then carefully applied some makeup to my face. It was no use though. No amount of makeup would hide the dark bruises. I'd just have to wait it out.

I went to the daybed and sat, propping the pillows up behind my head. Bringing my legs up, I extended them out in front of me. It felt amazing to stretch out. I leaned my head back and closed my eyes.

I had the sense of sleeping. Dreaming, as I approached a dense, dark pathway that seemed to go on forever. I wandered down the narrow trail, the grass brushing the tips of my fingers as I walked. It was quiet. No one else was around. It seemed too tranquil, a bit too safe. Something was wrong, yet I couldn't quite put my finger on it until I recognized the deep, rough voice. "You can't hide." I jerked my body around toward Troy ... he was alive. I ran that slow, sluggish jog you have during a dream, but my energy seemed too weak making my attempts at gaining enough speed to escape nearly impossible.

His voice was like a distant echo. "You can run, bitch, but you can't hide. I'll find you, and when I do, I'll kill you." I tripped over some shrubs. There was a creaking from a distance, moving closer, turning into scratching. I crawled my way through a thicket of thorny bushes as they scratched at my skin. Thorns tore at my clothes and arms; the warmth of blood seeped through my sleeve and trickled down my wrist. Then he grabbed me.

"Troy!" I screamed, shoving at the hands on my shoulders and pushing away from him, curling my body into the corner of the sofa. I held on to my knees, rocking. "He's dead, he has to be dead, please tell me he's dead."

"Shhh, you were dreaming." Jackson's voice sounded soothing, but as he reached for me, I curled further into myself. He stopped, held out his hand. "It's okay, he's not here. He can't hurt you now."

"No, you don't understand."

"What, Lena? What don't I understand? Tell me. I'll help you. Please trust me. I promise you can trust me."

I stared at his outstretched hand but didn't take it. I considered my dream a premonition. If I didn't kill Troy … "He'll kill me," I whispered loud enough for him to hear but not sure I wanted him to.

Jackson sat down beside me, and I rolled my knees up against my stomach. I hugged my arms around them, not ready to be close to anyone. Would I ever be?

We sat in silence for a moment. His fingers brushed against my arm and then he moved closer. I couldn't move. I was afraid to even breathe, and he probably sensed that since he didn't move either. Then a minute later, his arm moved behind me, and I let him pull me against him. I shivered under his arms as he held me tight. He rocked me, stroking my still damp hair. Maybe I was still dreaming. If this were real life, would I be letting a strange man hold me? Then, when Jackson asked "Who will kill you?", I realized his strong arms were real, and I very much wanted them to be safe.

I wanted to tell him what had happened as I sat secure in his embrace, not like Troy—nothing like Troy. I wanted to be able to trust someone. Still, how could I tell him that just that very morning I'd killed my husband? That I had his blood all over my hands when I ran, that I didn't look back and didn't call for help. I just left him there bleeding to death, I hoped. Did it make me a bad person that I hoped he was dead? I pushed myself away from Jackson's strong arms.

"I'm sorry. I shouldn't be putting all this on you. You don't even know me. You must think I'm horrible the way I walked into your place so early this morning all beat up." I swiped at the tears on my cheeks and sniffled as I sank back against the pillows.

"Listen, I want to help, really, but I understand your reluctance to confide in me. Hell, you don't know me from Adam, so if you don't feel like talking about it yet, that's okay. I'm ready to listen whenever you're ready. Look, are you hungry? I made some eggs and toast and a fresh pot of coffee. I thought maybe you'd like a bite to eat. There's not much food up here. Later, if you like—when you're feeling better—you can come down to my place, see if there are any staples you'd be interested in bringing up here. You know, tea, coffee, milk, sugar, cereal. Or if I don't have what you want or need, I can take you to the store, or better yet, go for you."

"What cloud did you say you were from?"

He laughed. "See that one over there?" He pointed out the window. "No, not that one," he said, as my gaze followed his, "the lighter one, over there. The one shaped like Pluto."

"The dog or the planet?"

"The dog, of course."

At that I smiled, and found myself relaxing a bit.

"Eat your eggs, you need your strength. I'll leave

you alone for a while to rest. Then you can expect me back to wake you up again. As Doc said, no more than two hours sleep at a time. Oh, here are two bags of ice. Keep one on your eye, and alternate the other between your side and your head."

As he began to get up from the daybed I realized I didn't want to be alone. The odds of Troy finding me, if he were alive, were slim, but I was afraid. I really should hate men and never want to be in the company of one again, except this man with his gentle green eyes and his soft voice soothed me. When he held me a few minutes ago, I wanted to stay there in his arms. I hadn't been joking when I asked him which cloud he came from. Because, truly, he must be an angel sent from heaven.

"Wait ... I know you probably have things to do, but please stay with me for a while. I don't want to be alone."

"Well, I do have to tend to some business ... but okay, I guess I can stay for a while. A short while. My brother—fully capable though he is—has a hard time holding it together without the knowledge that I'm right in the back room."

"You're kidding right?"

"Yeah, I'm kidding. Brodie is great. I don't know what I'd do without him. I like the idea of owning a bar, but I hate having to work in it."

I sat up a little, took a bite of the eggs and sipped some coffee. I hadn't realized I was hungry until then.

"Are you going to eat?" I didn't give him a chance to answer as I scooped up some eggs on the fork and held it in front of his lips. He opened his mouth and took the eggs. Funny, I'd never done that with Troy. Of course, Troy probably would have slapped me and accused me of forcing something on him he didn't want.

"Thanks, but I should be feeding you. You're the injured one," he said.

I picked up a slice of toast and before taking a bite, held it out for him. "Hey, you've done enough. And I know how to share."

He took a bite, and I took a bite, then I picked up the cup of coffee and sipped. We finished the eggs and toast together, and I leaned back against the pillows again putting one of the bags of ice to my eye and the other to my side, flinching from the chill. We stayed quiet for a few minutes, and I studied Jackson. I wanted to know what made him tick. He was awfully good looking. I loved the way his hair fell to his shoulders, and the way he was always brushing it back like he wasn't really used to it being that long. His eyes seemed to change color depending on the light. Hazel, I think it's called, but his leaned toward the green side more often than brown. He had a tiny scar under his right eye, and I had a sudden urge to touch it, maybe even kiss it, but kept my hands and my lips to myself. What was I thinking, anyway? Was it so wrong of me to be attracted to someone like him so soon after being beaten by Troy? I'd never met anyone like Jackson before. Someone who actually cared about what happened to me—a total stranger. Sure, Weezer and Gabby cared, but they knew me. Jackson just took me in; no questions asked.

"So, you own the bar, but you don't work at it. That's convenient. Just how did you manage that?"

"Ah." The green in his eyes brightened, he leaned back next to me, and my body tensed involuntarily. He had to have noticed, but didn't say anything. "Now that's a bit personal don't you think? I didn't know we had decided to share secrets yet."

I shrugged. "Okay, I get it, I tell you mine then you tell me yours, right?"

"Well, yeah. I mean if we're going to share secrets as well as breakfast."

I laughed but coughed at the same time. "Ow, ow, ow, that hurt."

"Oh, sorry sweetheart, I'll try not to make you laugh again. At least not for a few days, but I can't guarantee anything after that."

I thought about that for a minute. Where would I be in a few days when I was finally well enough to travel?

"It's funny. I hardly know you, but I feel as if I've known you for a long time. All the logic in the world tells me I shouldn't trust anyone, and I shouldn't *want* to be alone in the company of a man again, but I do feel comfortable here with you ... like this." I squeezed my eyes tight, realizing what I just revealed. I couldn't go on hiding my emotions in front of this guy. It was just too hard.

"So ... you weren't in an accident. It was a man who did this to you."

"I guess that was too easy for you. I haven't really been very consistent with my story. Yes, it was a man, although I'm not sure you could classify him as such."

"Ah, there I tend to agree with you. A man, a real man, would never hurt a woman that way." He reached out and took a couple strands of my hair, rubbing them between his thumb and forefinger. "Your hair is still a bit damp. Would you like me to dry it for you?"

"You want to dry my hair for me?"

"Yes. Wait, if memory serves, and the last tenant didn't take it there's a hair dryer here in this little bathroom."

He stood and went to the bathroom, returning a moment later holding a little red hair dryer and a brush.

"Um ... this is a little weird."

"If you think so." He set the dryer and brush down on the coffee table next to the tray of empty breakfast plates.

"Really, Jackson, I think I can dry my own hair." He plugged the dryer into the outlet behind the daybed and I picked up the brush. Lifting my arm up, taking one stroke down my head had me cringing in agony.

"Here. Let me help," he coaxed in a soft voice, taking the brush from my hand. "Your hair is making your shirt wet."

Could I really trust Jackson? I wanted to. It had been so long since I trusted anybody, except for Weezer, and even then it was only once. Troy kept too close an eye on me to try to talk to anyone, especially towards the end. "Well, okay. I wouldn't want the daybed to get all wet."

I managed to sit up and turn my back toward him, letting him stroke the brush through my tangled hair. He was gentle, careful not to pull. I closed my eyes and reveled in the attention. Never in my life had a man dried and brushed my hair for me.

The warm air from the dryer soothed me, and he was being careful not to let the heat stay in one spot too long. Not once did he put the brush near the bump on my head. My hair seemed to be dry. But he continued brushing and I caught myself grinning as his fingers ran through the strands behind each sweep of the brush. Maybe Troy did kill me and this was heaven.

I was going to have to talk about what happened sooner or later. Maybe it was best if I just got it over with now. Except right at this moment, I was enjoying the tenderness of Jackson's gentle hands.

Chapter 13

Jackson

I dried Lena's hair and brushed it until it was smooth, making careful short strokes starting at the end, and then longer ones as I got all the little tangles out. I made sure to be particularly cautious around the area by the bruise. After her hair was dry, I continued to brush the long strands, running my fingers through the silky threads behind each sweep of the brush. It was so satiny smooth and smelled like roses, a shampoo I'd found in Brodie's shower left by one of his female friends. *Mmmm ... good choice.*

"There, now you're almost perfect," I said softly.

"Almost," she said, gently touching the bottom part

of her eye as she sank back against the pillows.

I leaned back against the sofa, my arm resting by my leg, so close to the bottom of her feet. I moved it quickly on top of my thigh, not wanting to accidently rub against her skin. Those thoughts ran rampant in my brain, but I had to push them aside. I had more important things to concentrate on, like wanting to know about the creep she was running from, but I figured she'd never tell me until I gained her trust. I needed to give her time to recuperate.

I glanced at her. Her eyes were shut; her breathing relaxed. I watched as her chest rose with every breath she took, knowing each one probably hurt.

I carefully got up, pointed at Rufus and whispered, "Stay," and quietly let myself out, locking the door behind me. I had two sets of keys, and put this one on the key holder in the kitchen before I left. I went back to the bar to make good on my promise to Doc to buy him a beer. I wasn't looking forward to the twenty questions I knew would be waiting for me, not only from Doc, but from Brodie too.

I didn't want to stay too long. I needed to get back to wake Lena up. After I'd given Brodie and Doc the short version of what happened when I took her home, leaving out the bath and the hair drying, I had to endure listening to twenty minutes of taunting about the fawn and some other injured animals I'd rescued over the years. They'd managed to keep any mention of Lena out of the conversation in front of the rest of the guys in the bar. Both knew she was running from someone, and if word ever got out that I was helping a strange girl, well, you never know who might be listening.

I shrugged through most of it, laughing along until it wore me out and Brodie finally noticed my mood change to a somber one. "Sorry, Jackson," he said, patting me on the back. "Don't mind these guys, they're just having a little fun."

"Yeah, I know. Poke all you want. Wait until it's your dog or cat that needs rescuing, and see who's laughing then." I finished my coke, went to the office, grabbed my guitar, and took off. And for the first time in many years, I looked forward to going home.

Chapter 14

Lena

I awoke to the sound of birds chirping frantically just outside the window by the small kitchen. Jackson must have left it slightly open before he'd left because the room had smelled a bit musty when he first brought me up here. It had grown a bit chilly, so I got up and slowly walked over to the window to shut it when I saw the nest with three babies in it. The tiny birds sat nestled in a corner of the ledge just to my left under the eaves of the roof. It was just before dusk, and the three chicks chirped as though they'd been left alone all day long, and were famished. I knew the feeling.

Once, my mother had left me all day. I'd been

starving too by the time she finally came home just before midnight. I think I'd been around eight years old or close to that. We couldn't afford a babysitter, and she trusted me to stay at home alone for short periods of time after school so she could work a full eight-hour shift at the grocery store. When she came home that night, she'd apologized and said it had been out of her control. She said that the people at work needed her. She'd had a black eye, and when I questioned her about it she simply said it was an accident, and that I shouldn't worry about it. She'd promised never to leave me that long again, but taught me how to make a scrambled egg and toast just in case she was ever delayed like that again. By the time I was nine, I had dinner cooked for her almost every night. I was happy to do it. She worked hard, and I know she did it for me. She'd had a tough time of things most of her life, and told me she wanted me to be able to have the things she never had the chance to have.

Things changed though, once she married Carl. Then, she was home all the time. Except … she wasn't the same. She still loved me; I know she did, she just couldn't show me anymore. All her time had to be spent catering to Carl. Whatever Carl said, she did. Or else she'd get another one of those black eyes like the one she'd gotten when I was eight, and several times since, after she'd married Carl.

I loved my mother. I didn't want to be *like* her though. Unfortunately, soon after marrying Troy, I realized too late that I'd fallen down the same path that took my mother's life. I didn't believe in fate or destiny, and I certainly didn't believe in the theory that growing up in a battered home led to a battered life as an adult. With any luck, and a new view outside this window, I was on my way to changing my so-called destiny.

After closing the window, I turned to walk away and stubbed my toe on something. I looked down to see a metal hammer lying on the floor. I picked it up and glanced around the room wondering why Jackson had left it on the floor. There didn't appear to be any projects in the room that he'd been working on, but I guess he could have been working on just about anything that needed a hammer. I took it over to the daybed with me and placed it under the pillow before sitting down again.

No sooner had I settled back down when I heard a knock. I looked up and saw Jackson's smile through the glass window at the top of the door. I thought Jackson had a key, but I was pleased that he didn't just walk in. I'd had very jumpy nerves since earlier that morning, and I'm sure I would have freaked out if he'd just walked in.

"Come in," I said, but the door didn't open.

Instead, I heard, "I can't. I'm out of hands."

I giggled a little, and got up to open the door to find him standing there, a wide smile gracing his beautiful jaw as the smell of chicken soup wafted through the air. He balanced a tray with a bowl of soup and crackers, a sandwich with something that looked like meatloaf inside it, and a tall glass of milk on one palm. In the other, he held a couple of books.

"Hi," he said.

"Hi," I returned. He just stood there, balancing that tray, so I said, "Is that dinner?"

"Oh. Yeah." He laughed as he entered the room. He set the tray down on the table and simply stared at me. We stood in silence a moment before either one of us spoke.

"I thought you might be hungry," he finally said. "I'm actually a pretty good cook ... usually, but I ... I didn't have much time to go to the store today ... I mean, considering. That meatloaf is from last night. I hope you like meat ... I mean, I hope you eat it. I mean, meat."

I didn't say anything, mainly because he was kind of cute standing there fumbling over his words like a kid suddenly called upon to read his essay aloud to a room full of laughing teeny-boppers. You know, the one about what he did on his summer vacation, the vacation that ended with his first kiss. Then he added, "Meatloaf. I hope you like meatloaf."

"I do. Thanks." Jackson seemed a little different all of a sudden. Almost, shy. I didn't think of him as a shy man considering how he'd helped me so far, and I wondered what brought on the change. But when I looked down at myself, I realized the thermal shirt I wore adhered to my breasts as though it was molded to them, revealing my nipples. I quickly crossed my arms over my chest, and headed to the sofa. I didn't own a bra any longer, so I didn't know exactly how to fix the problem.

"I have a friend who is about your size," Jackson said. "Maybe she can lend you a … some clothes until we can get you some of your own. In the meantime, I'll … uh, be right back."

The quick sound of his footsteps on the stairs indicated he was running, and I guess I was right when he came back up, huffing out of breath, holding a terry robe out for me to put on.

"Thank you," I said, quickly shrugging into the soft blue material that not only hid my breasts, but also covered my hands since the sleeves fell two inches below them.

"Here, let me help," he said, taking one of the sleeves and rolling up the cuffs so that my hand appeared again. Then he did the same with the other one.

I smiled and sat, crossing my arms back over my chest. I felt very self-conscious now. I guess neither one of us had noticed before since I'd been sitting down the entire time. Plus, my back had been to him while he'd been brushing my hair.

"This all looks amazing. Thank you." I said, picking up the sandwich and taking a bite. "Mmmm, this is delicious," I said with a mouth full and covering my lips with my fingers while I chewed then swallowed. "Have you eaten?"

"Yeah. I have. I uh, need to get down to the house. I'll be back up later to check on you."

"Check on me?"

"Yeah, you know, no more than two hours sleep at a time—for tonight. After that, I think you'll be fine."

"Oh," I said, sounding a bit too disappointed, I thought. As much as I liked Jackson, I was glad he was leaving. Not that I didn't want his company, but I needed some time to get over the embarrassment of him seeing my breasts sticking to my shirt as if I'd been a contestant in wet T-shirt contest.

Chapter 15

Jackson

I'd never been so damn flustered in my whole life, but seeing Lena standing there with my shirt clinging to her breasts like that I'd lost my ability to speak. All I could think about was how perfect her breasts were, and I felt like a complete douche because I couldn't stop staring at them. I was supposed to be trying to gain her trust, not making her think I'm some perv. I should have tried harder to avert my eyes, but man, I am a full blooded twenty-two year old guy, complete with a high level of testosterone that always shows up when I least expect it. The sooner I got out of there, the better, for both our sakes.

SusanGriscom

Maybe Brodie and Doc were right, and I shouldn't get mixed up in this. Lena was a pretty girl under that bruised and beaten face. Somebody beat the crap out of her—a somebody who might come looking for her.

I paced the floor of the kitchen from one end to the other, running my hand through my hair as I thought. Let him come, I decided. Let him just try to lay another hand on her and see how far he gets. When I get through with him, he won't be able to use those hands for a long time for anything, not even to get his own rocks off.

I swiveled my body, swinging my fist out through the air, just missing Brodie's jaw by inches as he jumped back.

"Whoa, bro. What's up?"

"Nothing. I'm just ready to pound the asswipe who decorated Le … Lana's face, and used her body as a doormat for kicking the shit off his boots."

"What? Did she tell you who it was?"

"No, but when I find out … I'm going to make him wish he'd never met her."

"I hope you're just blowing smoke, because you, more than anyone, should know what could happen if you lay a hand on that creep."

"That's only if he can prove I threw the first punch."

"Yeah? And who's to say he couldn't. Lana? Don't count on it. Women like her always end up sticking up for the creep who'd beat them. You know that."

I grabbed the collar of my brother's shirt and

88

shoved him against the wall. "Don't talk about her that way. She's not like those other women who keep going back to the bastards who beat them time and time again, defending the S.O.Bs like they're mini-gods."

"How do you know? You've known her for what, ten hours?"

"I just know." I shook my head, let go of his shirt and stepped back.

"Shit. You're falling for her. Already? Don't be stupid, Jack."

I shot him a dagger riddled stare, but he continued anyway. "I'm not saying anything you don't already know. She might be a nice girl."

"She is!"

"Okay, but … look, I didn't mean to imply she wasn't nice. I'm just saying what usually happens in abuse cases. If it was abuse." I glared at him again. "I suppose it could have been rape. Then, of course, she wouldn't defend the guy. All I'm saying is be careful, Jackson. It seems to me that anyone mean enough to do what he did to Lana would go out of his way to get you thrown in jail for messing with even one strand of his hair. Plus, abused women usually defend the abuser. If it was abuse, we've seen it before, right here in our own little town, Jack."

Brodie was right. We had seen it with our own uncle. Late one night, right before last call, a man and woman were arguing. It suddenly got more heated and turned ugly, with the guy striking the woman and knocking her four feet back into the bar until Uncle Joe stepped in to defend her. Joe was a big man, and had no problem beating the guy until he was out cold. Broke his nose, too. The cops came, and the woman took her boyfriend's side, accusing Uncle Joe of starting the fight. It was their word against his since there were no other witnesses, and Uncle Joe spent the next six months in jail for battery and assault. I didn't want a repeat of that.

"I know you're right, but don't let it go to your head."

He laughed. "Don't worry, big brother, you'll always be the one I look up to."

It was past midnight, and I'd left Lena alone for too long. If she fell asleep, and I didn't wake her, and if she did have a concussion, she could lapse into a coma; though I honestly didn't think that would happen. She seemed too alert for one thing. Secondly, she didn't have any other symptoms like vomiting, which usually accompanied a concussion. I liked the idea of checking on her every couple of hours anyway.

The lights were off inside the rental so I figured she was asleep. I didn't want to scare her awake by knocking on the door, so I used my key and let myself inside. I felt as if I were trespassing or invading her privacy, but I figured she knew I'd be coming up again to check on her. She lay on the daybed on her side; her bruised eye hidden against the pillow. Her other eye was closed, and she looked very much like an angel. She was beautiful. As I approached her side, she stirred a little, then sprang up and screamed. Pulling a hammer out from under her pillow, she raised it in the air ready to strike at me. I thought she was going to kill me.

"It's just me! Don't hit me," I said, grabbing her arm, holding it steady as I coaxed the hammer out of her hand and into mine.

"Oh, Jackson, I'm sorry. I thought you were … I didn't realize it was you."

"I guess I don't have to worry about you defending yourself."

"I found the hammer on the floor over by the window. I felt more secure with it under my pillow."

"I must have left the hammer there after I fixed some loose floorboards last week. I should have known I'd frighten the living daylights out of you, coming into a dark room to wake you up that way. I'm sorry."

"No, please. No need to apologize."

I set the hammer down on the table in front of her, in case she wanted to put it back under her pillow after I left. If that's what made her feel secure, then it was fine by me, as long as she didn't use it on my head.

The next day went a bit smoother since I didn't need to wake Lena up every couple of hours. I didn't have many excuses to visit her up there, other than bringing her food, though. I decided not to go back up during that first night when she almost bashed my head in. I knew she didn't have a concussion, and I'd only been using it as an excuse to spend time with her.

I brought her breakfast again, the same as I had the past couple of days. I knocked on the door, and a couple of seconds later the latch clicked. She inched the door open holding the robe I gave her closed tightly in her fist.

"Breakfast is served." I smiled the best classy grin I could muster, and she smiled back, taking a step to the side as she opened the door wide enough for me to enter.

"You didn't mention that the room included room service every day. I might have to start figuring out some way to give you a tip."

I paused and shot her a quick glance, trying not to look so shocked at her statement, figuring she didn't realize the implications of what she'd just said. I cleared my throat. "No tipping is necessary," I said, but secretly wished I could take her up on her offer. Maybe someday, if she ever recovered from the horrible experience she'd been through.

I sat with her as she ate, and she insisted on sharing it with me again. "I should have just brought up two plates," I said. "Maybe if we can get you some better clothes, you could come down to the house and have a proper meal with us."

"That would be nice." She smiled and popped the last of the toast into her mouth.

"I'll work on that today. I'm sure Brodie can come

up with some clothes."

I wanted her to tell me what had happened, who had hurt her. I couldn't help her if she didn't confide in me, so I took a chance and brought up the subject.

"The other day, after your nightmare, you mentioned the guy that hurt you. You made a statement about him not being a real man. Let's get back to this not-a-real-man that made mincemeat of your face—not to mention your body—who is he?"

Lena sighed and pulled her legs up on the sofa beside her. "I'm afraid to tell you."

"Please, tell me. I promise you can trust me." I leaned back against the sofa at the other end. Her legs were curled up so that the balls of her feet rested slightly against my thigh. I wanted to pick her feet up and massage them, but it was probably too soon for something as intimate as rubbing her feet.

She reached for the cup of coffee from the table and took a sip, then stared into the black liquid as if the words she needed would somehow pop up to the surface like in some alphabet soup. Then she finally said, "This is hard, but you've been so nice I feel I owe you some explanation. I just need a minute."

"Okay," I said. "Take your time."

Silence hummed in the air for several seconds, then the words I'd most feared flowed from her lips in almost a whisper.

"My husband."

Chapter 16

Lena

Jackson didn't get up. He didn't walk out. He didn't yell at me and tell me I was stupid. He just sat at the other end of the sofa, allowing my feet to stay warm against his thigh. I wondered if he realized that. His body stiffened a little when I said "my husband", but other than that and a small twitch in his jaw, he made no other movement. I wanted to tell him. I needed to tell somebody. So far, Jackson had done nothing to make me believe I couldn't trust him. But I trusted Troy at one time, too. Was Jackson the right person? Would he turn me in to the cops if I told him the rest of my secret? That was a chance I decided I needed to take, only because I did trust him.

When Jackson didn't say anything, I thought he might be getting ready to leave after all. I could have been mistaken about his reaction. His silence made all sorts of things run through my mind, and I was suddenly sorry I'd told him who it was. But then Jackson did something. He stroked his thumb and finger along the edge of his jaw and glanced at me, giving me a brief but caring smile, still not saying anything, but the movement and the smile gave me encouragement to go on.

I moved my legs off the sofa and sat up straight, needing to be in a less vulnerable position. "Jackson?"

"Yes?"

"I think I killed him."

The twitch in his jaw became stronger as his body flinched again. He stood, walked to the window and stared out. Neither of us said anything for what felt like a full two minutes, when Jackson finally spoke.

"How?" he whispered, keeping his eyes outside. I wondered if he was watching the baby birds or thinking about what I'd said.

"I stabbed him in the stomach."

He turned and gave me a shocked look. "During his attack?" I wanted to crawl under the rug and hide from his sight. This was all too demoralizing. I am a murderer, and now Jackson surely must think the worst of me.

"Yes," I said and left it at that. I couldn't go on

with the rest of the horrible story.

Jackson nodded, came back to the couch, and sat beside me, his hands in his lap. "That must have been very scary." A grim, contemplating frown marred his features, and he stared straight ahead. I thought he would be horrified, but Jackson seemed to possess a quality that made me almost feel okay about what I'd done.

"Would you like to tell me about it? I mean, it might help to talk about it."

I closed my eyes, remembering how it all happened. I was about to tell him everything, and I wanted to make sure I had all the facts straight. For the first time in a very long time, I really did feel safe. I thought about the horrible man Troy had become, not the man I married. I thought about the difference between him and Jackson, or even Doc, and I knew I'd made a good decision to run. Jackson sat close to me, but not close enough to touch me or make me feel uncomfortable.

"He came home drunk," I began. "He started beating on me because he couldn't ... you know," I made an up and down gesture with my hands, a little embarrassed to say the words, but finally managed a barely audible, "Get it up."

Jackson gave me a short smile, but quickly became serious again, so I continued. "After he'd punched me, thrown me against the wall, and kicked me a few times in the side, he stopped. I'm sure it was more of a pause in the punishment, which is what he called it because I knew he'd be back to complete the job. He left me on the floor in the bedroom, and when he went to the toilet, I somehow managed to get up and drag myself downstairs to the kitchen. I grabbed a small steak knife out of the drawer. God, if he knew I had that knife in my hand—"

Tears stung my eyes as I wiped at them with the heel of my hand and continued. "He told me he was sorry and stood real close to me. I remember my fingers sweating around the knife, and I was afraid I would drop it. I was so scared. He put his hands on my shoulders, then moved them to my neck and started choking me. I couldn't breathe, Jackson. I couldn't get any air in. I didn't know what else to do, so I stabbed him."

Jackson's arms were around me, rubbing my arm, my back. "I'm so sorry, Lena." That was all Jackson said for the longest time while I sobbed against his chest. When I picked my head up, he titled up my chin and said, "That must have been very hard to do. I'm glad you were so brave."

Brave? He was calling me brave after I just told him I'd killed Troy. "How does murder equate to bravery?" I managed to ask.

"That wasn't murder. That was self-defense. Are you sure he was dead?"

"Yes … no. I think so."

"Well, given the state you were in when you walked into my bar, and the way you were dressed, I can only assume that you left there quickly. Did you check to see if he was actually dead? Check for a pulse?

"I was afraid to touch him, in case he wasn't. I didn't want him to grab me."

"Okay. I can understand that. Did you call the police?"

"I couldn't call the cops, he'd made sure of that."

"And how would that be?" His voice still sounded soft, still steady, and I took comfort in it. It gave me the courage to go on with the tale.

"Earlier this year he had me arrested for assault and battery."

"What? How?"

"I hit him with a bat and broke his jaw."

"Good for you."

"Yeah, well it was an accident, at least on my part. He walked into it on purpose. He was showing me how to hit a ball, and when I swung the bat he stepped into it. Then he accused *me* of doing it on purpose, and had me arrested so I would have an assault and battery record, and would never be able to accuse him of hurting me."

I expected Jackson to tell me how stupid I'd been to believe him. I still don't know if it was true or not, but I didn't want to take any chances with the law. I suppose I could have looked it up or asked someone, but I didn't want to raise any suspicions. When Jackson didn't argue or tell me I was stupid, I still felt the need to defend myself, regardless.

"We didn't have a computer. I couldn't look up

any information about that. Troy had forbidden computers in the house. He said he didn't want one of those wives that sat around all day chit chatting with her friends on Facebook."

"No doubt to keep you from telling anyone about how he was treating you," Jackson added.

"Not that I would have. He would have found out, and probably killed me. There wasn't much I could keep from him, and from what I know about computers it's difficult to hide things from one another, even with passwords. Look, Jackson, I don't pretend to think that I wasn't stupid to let him run my life the way he did. It just happened so quickly. I thought we were happy. He was … everything. Until right after we were married. He completely changed. I never saw it coming."

"I don't think you were stupid, Lena, not at all. I do believe you were scared though, and I hate that you had to go through that."

Sitting here telling Jackson the story made it all seem so surreal, like some movie on the Lifetime channel. "Troy convinced me to run off to Las Vegas with him and get married. I'd only known him about a month. Everyone said I should wait, but I thought I knew him. Then, two weeks after the wedding he struck me for the first time. We'd been out partying with my friends from the band, celebrating our marriage, drinking and dancing, having a great time. I thought. Troy liked my friends; at least he always seemed to. Anyway, I'd danced with my friend Weezer that night.

It was a slow dance. He wanted to talk to me privately, to make sure I was doing okay since Troy and I ran off and got married without letting anyone know. He was concerned, said he hadn't trusted Troy in the beginning, but I reassured him I was fine. That satisfied him, I guess, and he said if I was happy that's all that mattered.

Troy drank a lot, and later that night after we'd gotten home we argued about me dancing with Weezer. He accused me of wanting to be with Weezer, and slapped me across the face. Then he yanked his wedding ring off and chucked it across the room. He said he didn't want to be married to me anymore if I was going to act like a slut and a whore every time we went out with my friends. I'd been horrified, and afraid he'd hit me again, but relieved when he'd stumbled into the bed and promptly fell asleep. I was heartbroken, and ended up crying myself to sleep that night. In the morning, he'd apologized, saying how sorry he was, begging me to forgive him and saying that he didn't know what came over him. We spent the morning searching the room for his wedding ring. When we found it, he kissed me and promised never to take it off again. He also promised that he would never hit me again." False promises. I should have known, just like my stepfather. I kept that last part to myself, not wanting to get into a conversation about my *awesome* childhood.

"You say they were *your* friends, but how did you meet Troy?"

"One of the guys in the band, Phil, introduced us. Phil said he'd known Troy in high school. They'd been in the same English class as juniors. I don't think he really knew Troy, or remembered much about him from high school, though. I think they happened to run into each other one night after one of our gigs. I remember seeing Troy approach Phil, and they started talking like long lost buddies, reminiscing about school and stuff. I thought Troy was handsome and sweet at the time. He swept me off my feet."

"That sounds fairly familiar. You shouldn't feel bad about trusting the guy if you had a friend who'd known him. I've had that happen—the long lost friend from high school making a sudden appearance back in my life. Of course, the guy didn't turn out to be some psycho nut-job."

I forced a smile at what Jackson said, appreciating his understanding.

"So, it was bad from the beginning?" he asked.

"Not really. Everything was fine for a few weeks. I thought that night he'd slapped me was a one-time occurrence, and he'd only hit me because he'd been drunk and jealous. About a month after that he came home from work one night, grumpy and swearing about something that had happened at the job site. He worked in construction, and he'd been replaced as foreman on the project. I knew he was upset, so I stayed quiet and listened with great interest, wanting to support him as much as possible. He ranted about how unfair the whole thing had been, and how he deserved to be foreman; that the new one didn't know jack shit. The awful day he'd had at work must have set him off. The blow to my cheek had been completely unexpected, came out of nowhere. I'd set dinner on the table and was getting ready to sit down, when he got up from his chair and backhanded me across the face. He said his meat was too tough, and I needed to learn how to cook. That night he told me each time I made him something he didn't like, he would reward me with a slap until I learned to do it right. That's when he made me quit the band and all my friends. He blamed them for my lack of attention to detail. He said I needed to stay home and take care of him like a good wife. The next day he gave me a new cell phone and programmed it so he could see everywhere I went. If I didn't take it with me when I went out, he'd have known. He called me every hour, sometimes, twice. He was never consistent, so it was difficult to know when he would check up on me."

I lowered my face into my hands. "God, I don't know how I let it all happen. I'd always thought of myself as being smarter than that. I wanted to leave him when I figured out the life I'd gotten myself into. I would have left him sooner, but he threatened to hunt me down and kill me if I ever tried to leave him. I was pathetic, scared."

I stopped talking and sucked in a sob. I thought of my mom. Was that what had happened to her?

"Had you ever given any thought to a shelter for battered women?"

"Of course. Except, he'd find me at one of those. He knew all about them, in fact, reminded me often that I should never try to go to one because a shelter would be the first place he would check. He also told me they'd never believe me anyway considering it was his nose that hit the bat I had held. He would have found me, stalked me, and terrorized me until I came home. He told me he would.

"The first time Troy hit me I thought maybe I deserved it for making him jealous. But the second time, I told myself I would never let him do that again. I would have left then, but I didn't have any money, and I had nowhere to go. If I'd gone to a friend's he would have found me. Everything was in his name, credit cards, even bank accounts, and shortly after that was when he had me arrested. I knew if I ran he would come after me. I had to get away from him, but I also knew he would never let me go."

"You were more of a prisoner than a wife," Jackson said in a quiet, thoughtful voice. "But in a shelter you would receive safety, support, and get a fresh start on life. Maybe even make a few friends there with women who are in the same boat as you."

"No!" I shouted the word, and instantly regretted the way it came out. "No, I can't go to a shelter. I won't go. I'd rather stay running for the rest of my life than take a chance that he would find me."

"Well, I know shelters are safer than what he told you. You would be very safe, but I can respect your desire not to go to one."

"Thank you. I did start making plans, though. I saved money, even got a fake ID. I was going to sneak away when I had enough money saved. I never intended to kill him, but he would have killed me if I hadn't. I believe that. I know I panicked, but don't you see? Stupid or not, I had no choice."

"I don't think you're stupid, Lena. Scared, yes, but not stupid. We need to find out if he is still alive or not."

"Yeah, but I can't. If he is dead, I'll be arrested for murder, and if he's not dead, he'll find me, and then I'll be dead."

"No, he won't kill you. I won't let him. And as far as you committing murder? Not a chance. One look at you, and any cop would know what happened."

"God, no. Please, Jackson, I can't involve the cops. I know you want to help, and I appreciate it. I appreciate everything you've done so far, but I'll need to leave just as soon as I can."

Chapter 17

Jackson

"No!" I practically shouted the word. "I can help you. Let me."

"I know what's going to happen. My mother, she went to jail. She went to jail for two years for shooting my stepfather, and he hadn't even died. She'd had bruises on her as well, and when she got out of jail he found us and killed her. The police didn't believe my mother's story, why would they believe mine?" She sobbed, and her body shook. "I knew I shouldn't have told you. Please, don't turn me in."

"Shhhh, shhhh." I stroked her hair and held her close. "Lena, trust me, I won't turn you in, but I will help you get through this. I promise. How about you try and get some rest now."

She nodded and leaned back on the pillow, draping her arm across her forehead. "I'll try, but please, you promised, no cops."

"I promise."

I would keep my promise and not involve the police, but I couldn't just sit back and do nothing. This time when she fell asleep I took the liberty of looking in her purse for some identification. I felt horrible about snooping in her things like that, but I didn't think she'd give me her last name considering how scared she was, and I needed to know if I was going to help her. I found three IDs: one said, Lana Martin, one Lena Harington. The third one had expired a year ago, and the name on it was Lena Benton, most likely her maiden name. Lana was her fake name, and she'd told me the ass-wipe's first name, in addition to shouting the name out in her dream. Troy. I assumed that her husband's full name must be Troy Harington.

Leaving Lena there on the bed to sleep, I went down to the main house. I had to find out if her husband was dead or alive. If he was dead, I had to find a way to talk Lena into confessing. I knew that would be going back on my word, but I had no intention of aiding and abetting or harboring a fugitive—not that I considered her a fugitive; I didn't think she was guilty of anything except being scared—but if she didn't turn herself in, then she damn well would be, and I sure as hell didn't want to be a fugitive myself. I'd never call the cops directly. I'd keep that part of my promise for sure. If she did manage to kill the S.O.B., I'd try my damndest to convince her to do the right thing.

The address on the Lena Harington ID was in Medford, Oregon. She'd mentioned Medford that very first day, but never really said that was where she was from, so I hoped the ID was current.

Unfortunately, it wasn't. After an extensive search on the internet, where I accessed several different background checking services, I found that out. So I did a wide area search for a Troy Harington in cities six hours away in all four directions. I came up with twelve individuals with the name Troy Harington. One was just a small boy of six—that ruled him out—one an older man of fifty-five, residing in Brookings. I didn't think Lena would be married to someone that old, but one never knew. I continued down the list, checking the ages of each person. Most were middle aged, but the seventh Troy Harington on the list looked promising—a twenty-three-year old construction worker residing in Medford. Nice of him to advertise I thought as I studied the resume. The jerk never bothered to remove it after he found employment.

His current employer was Smith and Trent Building Association.

I made a call to my friend Luke Preston, a guy I'd gone to college with. Luke was now an attorney based out of Portland. The guy was a genius who had managed to graduate and pass the bar all before he turned twenty-four. Though Luke was a few years older than me, we'd hit it off immediately, and seemed to find ourselves hanging out together at those all night frat parties at the house. It was nice hanging with a senior, especially one with a lot of connections. I was just a freshman—a younger than most freshman at that, and Luke got me into most of the clubs without questions about I.D. At barely seventeen I didn't possess one for legally drinking, of course, so it was nice to have him on my side.

"Sharper, Lloyd, and Preston. How may I help you?" a sweet, smooth voice sang through the portable phone I held to my ear.

"Yes, I'd like to speak with Luke Preston," I told the lady on the other end.

"May I tell him who is calling?"

"Jackson Beaumont."

She put me on hold, and within a few seconds, Luke came on the line. "Hey, Jackie, how the hell are you?"

"Great, great."

"Still running your uncle's pub outside of Redding?"

"Yep, and still enjoying watching my brother work his tail off in it."

"Well, hey, when you grow tired of that tough life you let me know, we still have room for another great attorney here—providing you pass the bar."

"Ha ha, thanks. Keep dreaming. I need a favor."

"Anything for a fraternity brother pal, you know

that."

"Yeah, that's why I called you. Anyway, could you check on a guy named Troy Harington? He lives in Medford, Oregon. Works in construction, I think. See if he's still living in the area, and see if he's showed up for work, um … since, last Tuesday, I think. He works for a small construction firm, Smith and Trent."

"Sure, but can't you do that yourself?"

"I could, but it's complicated. It would be better if you did it from there. I don't want the guy to find out I'm the one checking."

As much as I trusted Luke, I didn't want to give him any more information just yet, and if Troy was still alive, I didn't want to raise any flags and have Troy trace me to Lena. The fright emanating from that girl's mind was way too strong.

"Okay, Jack, give me thirty minutes and I'll get back to you."

"Great. And Luke, keep this under the radar will you?"

"Sure, sure, no problem, talk to you in a few."

I hung up and called Brodie.

"Brodie, how's it going?" I considered asking Brodie to call one of his cuties to borrow some clothes for Lena, and then decided to just buy her something new instead. That would be better, the fewer people that knew about her the better.

"Good, not too busy here, are you coming in today?"

"Not today, maybe tonight. I haven't decided yet."

"Oh, your 'fawn' keeping you occupied, I guess." I could picture Brodie's eyebrows wiggling as he made his little joke.

"Yeah, you could say that. Listen, I know I told you this before, but I want to make sure, don't tell anyone about Lana, okay? And if anyone comes in asking about her or someone that looks like her, well, you don't know anything and never saw her."

"Jack, what's going on? Is she in some sort of trouble?"

"You might say that."

"It's more than just abuse isn't it?"

"Yeah, I'll fill you in some other time."

"Jack."

"Yeah Brodie, I know, I'll be careful."

I no sooner hung up from calling Brodie, when the phone rang again. It was Luke.

"Hey Jack, I got some information on that guy you asked about. Troy Harington. He didn't show up to work last Tuesday or Wednesday." My heart sank to the bottom of my chest.

"He called in sick, said he had the flu."

"Really?" I said, full of new hope. "Then he's alive."

"What do you mean, 'then he's alive?' What have you gotten yourself mixed up in?"

"Me? Nothing. I'm just looking out for a friend of mine. A girl. It's just good to hear he's okay."

"Yeah, funny thing is though, his boss said he

heard the sound of voices over a loud speaker in the background when he'd called in sick. He said it sounded a lot like hospital voices. He asked if he was in the hospital, but Troy said no. I made a couple of calls to several of the local emergency rooms. Medford Mercy told me he'd been in there with a wound to the side of his abdomen, just missing his liver; it took the doctor fourteen stitches to sew him up. The guy said a garage door hinge flew into him while he was doing a repair on it. Came in with the metal still stuck in his gut."

"Thanks, Luke. Out of curiosity, how did you get Mercy hospital to give you the information on him?"

"Oh, good thing for you, I sort of have a thing going on with a cute little nurse over there. She said the guy was a real jerk. 'Scum of the earth' were her exact words. What's this about, Jackson? You can trust me. You know I'll help in any way I can."

"Yeah, I know. This guy beat up on a friend of mine. He's her husband. She's young, scared, and doesn't want to press charges."

"Okay. Well, I know she's in good hands with you. Let me know if she decides to file a complaint. Sounds like she needs a divorce, too."

"Yeah." Wouldn't that be nice, I thought. "Thanks, Luke. I owe you one. I'll call you to file a restraining order against the guy just as soon as I get some pictures and a police report filed if she agrees."

"No problem. Hey, it sounds like you're looking to

get into the P.I. business. What's the matter, the music world not cutting it for you?"

"Naw. Music's my life. You know that. I'm just looking out for a friend. I'll try and email those pictures to you by this afternoon."

"I knew there had to be a female in the mix here somewhere. Keep me posted," Luke said, chuckling as he hung up the phone.

Well, great! Lena didn't kill the bastard. Unfortunately, though, she was married—to a scumbag—but still, married. Now I had to find a way to tell her so she wouldn't be upset with me for checking.

Before I knew it, two hours had gone by. I went upstairs to check on Lena. I peeked in through the glass. She was still sound asleep and looked like an angel as she lay there with Rosie sleeping under her arm and Rufus down at the other end on top of her feet. I hated to disturb her, so I turned to leave when I heard her call my name.

"Jackson?"

I used my key and opened the door. "Yeah. Hey, I ah … wanted to know if you wanted something to eat, but I thought you were still sleeping. I didn't want to disturb you."

"Yeah, I saw you peeking in. Thanks, but I'm not very hungry right now." She reached behind her and pulled out the plastic bag that once held ice, now just a bag of water. "Hey, let me get you some more ice. It's good that you've been applying it so often. It looks like it's helping a lot. Your eye isn't nearly as bad as it was a couple of days ago." I picked up the baggie and stopped. "Do you think I could borrow that hammer you have stashed under your pillow?"

"She smiled. "Sure."

She handed me the hammer, and I went to fill the baggie with ice cubes, crushing them down to small chips so they would be easier to manipulate and less bumpy against her eye.

"Here, place this on your eye for a while."

"Thanks," she said when I handed her the new cold bag of ice. "I've been applying it about three times a day. The sooner I can go out in public, the sooner I can pay you."

She rubbed her hand over her forehead before sinking back down so the ice bag could rest over her eye. She looked sleepy, laying there staring up at me with one eye. I dreaded telling her what I knew, and I figured she would be furious with me, but I couldn't let her continue to believe she actually killed her husband.

"Lena," I said, and she looked up at me with that one groggy, sad eye. I changed my mind. This girl had enough pain going on right now. What I had to tell her would only make her angry and hurt that I betrayed her. I couldn't tell her yet. I needed more time to get her to trust me.

"What is it?" she asked, and winced as she repositioned her still injured body on the sofa as if trying to alleviate some of the pain in her side.

"Are you comfortable here?" A stupid question,

considering how much pain she was in, but it was all I could come up with, and I didn't want to continue with what I had originally intended to tell her.

She gave me a half smile. "Yes. Thank you. This is more than I could have hoped for."

"Okay. Good. You stay as long as you want, then."

"Well, I will pay you, as soon as I get back on my feet and I'm able to earn some money."

"I know. I have faith in you." And I did. I would give her another day or two to get to know me and trust me more, before probing her with questions as well as revealing my betrayal. "Do you need anything before I go back downstairs?"

"No, I'm fine for now."

"I'll come back up and bring you something to eat a little later on."

Every time I went up to see Lena or bring her something, I stayed to talk. I enjoyed her company, and I hoped she was enjoying mine. I hated lying to her about her husband. Keeping up the ruse of not knowing whether she killed him or not grated on my conscience, especially the way she continued to agonize over the act. Lena was not a killer, but she believed with all her soul that she was. Today, I decided I would change that.

She sat in her usual spot on the daybed, and I sat down at the other end, but I didn't feel comfortable there. I needed to be facing her, so I got up and sat on the coffee table in front of her.

"Lena, I know you'll be pissed, and I'm sorry."

Her eyes grew wide with fear. "What did you do?"

"I … ah … I'm sorry, but I took the liberty of doing some checking while you were sleeping yesterday, and I had to go through your purse to do it." Her mouth gaped open, and I held up my hands, palms out, when she started to object. "Sorry, I needed your last name. I called a friend of mine that I went to school with, Luke. He's an attorney residing in Portland. He checked on Troy Harington—that is your husband, right?"

"Oh no! You didn't! You promised! I need to get out of here." She sat up, looking as if she wanted to bolt, but I didn't think she really had the strength, and she remained seated. "How could you? I trusted you."

"Please, you *can* trust me. You're safe here. I trust Luke. He would never betray me."

"You turned me in."

"No! I didn't." Shit. Agitated, I ran my hand through my hair. The last thing I wanted was for her to lose trust in me.

"But the police, they'll find me now."

"That's what I'm trying to tell you. The police aren't looking for you."

"How do you know?"

"Because Troy is still alive. You didn't kill him, so you can relax."

"He's alive?" Lena closed her eyes and sank back against the sofa. "That's even worse."

"No, it's going to be okay."

"How did you find this out?"

"I have resources. My buddy, Luke, the attorney I know, checked with his work. Troy called in sick the morning you stabbed him, but his boss said he sounded as if he was calling from a hospital. Luke called around to a few emergency rooms. He got lucky when he called a girlfriend of his that works at Medford Mercy. She told him that Troy had been in there needing stitches in his stomach. Apparently, he told the doctors he had some sort of accident while repairing a garage door. So, you're completely in the clear."

She didn't exactly look thrilled. In fact, she started to cry. "It would be better if he were dead. Now I have to keep running. I'd rather go to jail. At least I'd stay alive there."

"Lena, I won't let him find you. I won't let him hurt you. You need to trust me. You won't go to jail for stabbing him either. You were defending yourself. We can have him picked up for beating you. He won't have a chance once the police see you. They *will* believe you. I promise."

"No. You don't understand. Even if he goes to jail now, he'll get out eventually, and he'll come after me. The only thing we'll accomplish is making him madder."

"Okay, we'll do it your way. We won't have him picked up, but let me file a police report just so we have proof that he beat you. And at least let me help you file for a divorce. You can stay hidden; he won't find you here."

"How can I stay hidden if I file for a divorce?"

I scooted next to Lena and put my arm around her shoulder. She flinched a little, but I left it there anyway. I needed her to trust me, and the best way I knew how to do that was to let her realize I wouldn't hurt her. I didn't want her to go through the rest of her life being afraid of men, me in particular.

"Well, I may appear to be your average Joe bartender, but underneath all this ..." I gestured to myself by splaying my fingers out and let my hand flow down in front of me from my head to my waist. "I do know something about the law. So, I guess it's my turn to tell you something about me. I said I'd tell you my secret if you told me yours, so here goes. I was going to be an attorney. My parents wanted—or my mother wanted—me to be an attorney. I graduated college, but never continued on with law school. Brodie talked me into joining the police department with him instead. Told me I was too tough to be a lawyer, and that I should be a cop with him. My brother knows me pretty well; we both knew I'd hate sitting in an office. We joined the police department, went through the academy together. We were both cops for a while. One day I got this wild hair up my ass and decided police work was too unforgiving, too violent. I'm an extremely placid guy, can't handle too much violence. Anyway, I talked Brodie into going into business with me, to become Private Investigators and move out of the city. Sounded like a great idea to him. We grew up out here in this town, and we had both grown tired of the hustle and bustle of big city life, so we came back home. The thing is that there's not too many people out here who need a good PI."

I shifted around so she could lean against me now that she seemed more relaxed.

"I acquired the bar from my Uncle Joe a year ago. He died and left everything he had to my brother and me. My brother got his house, and I got the bar. I'm not sure why he did it that way, but he made a stipulation in his will that I couldn't sell the bar for at least ten years. I guess my uncle knew me better than I knew myself. I hated what I was doing, the investigative work. The little work we did find turned out to be in nearby cities, and was mostly spying on cheating spouses, and those weren't frequent enough to pay any bills. This is a small, sleepy town, and everyone knows everyone, so there was never any P. I. work around here. I tried working the bar by myself, but I was more interested in playing with the band, so Brodie volunteered to do most of the bartending. Seems he needed something to do with his time too since our Private Investigating firm went belly-up. Plus he figured it was a great way to meet the ladies. Unfortunately for him, this is a small town, and there aren't very many ladies around. But he's okay with it. He claims that the ones that come passing through are perfect. No strings attached. He's been sort of on these one night stand kicks now since … well, anyway, he's not really in a good frame of mind for getting involved right now. That's the way he likes it. So, we still have our P. I. license, but as I said, it's not a thriving business. My friend, Luke, in Portland, specializes in family law. He can file the papers for you, and Troy will never know where you are." When she remained silent, I grew concerned. "You do want a divorce don't you?"

"Troy will never agree to a divorce."

Chapter 18
Lena

"He doesn't have to agree," Jackson countered so quickly it was as if he'd had the words on the tip of his tongue before I had a chance to make the statement. "Oregon is a no fault divorce state, just like California. All you have to do is state irreconcilable differences. The fact that you want a divorce, and he doesn't, is sufficient. It is considered an irreconcilable difference. He can't object to a divorce. He can only dispute the terms, such as custody and property division."

"Well, there's no custody battle since we didn't have any kids, and we didn't own our house, but he'll never sign the papers. He told me that."

"He doesn't need to sign the papers. If he won't cooperate you can get a divorce by what's called—defaulting your spouse."

"What does that mean?"

"It means we file a divorce petition, and have him served. With or without his blessing, we get an order from the court barring him from objecting to the divorce, and then ninety days after that we'll submit a final judgment of divorce, with or without his signature. Even if he objects and files a response, the judge can, and will, order a divorce over his objection."

"You can really do this for me without him knowing where I am?"

"Yes."

"My God, I've been so stupid."

"No, you've been scared, that's all."

"Right. I was too scared to even investigate the possibility of divorce. I've been scared to breathe. It's taken me a whole year to save money and get the courage to leave. If he hadn't beaten me so badly the other morning, I would still be there."

A shiver crawled up from the bottom of my toes and settled at the base of my skull.

"But you did get out. You had to endure hell first, but you did get out. That takes courage. You should be proud of yourself."

"This all sounds great, and I really appreciate it. You've been ... you are wonderful. But ... he'll never give up. He'll never quit looking for me."

Jackson straightened and turned to face me, taking my hands in his. "Lena, I'm not going to try to sugarcoat this. You're right; he will look for you. That's why we need to take every precaution we can to make sure that doesn't happen, starting with you telling me every move you made from the time you stabbed him. I also need to take some pictures of your bruises. Is that okay?"

"Pictures, why?"

"We need to press charges and file a restraining order against him, that's why. Not that that's going to keep him from trying to get at you. If he's anything like most abusers, he will keep trying. In his mind, you are his property, and he won't stop hunting you."

"I'm scared, Jackson. I don't think I can do this." I wanted to get in my car and drive. I didn't know to where, just away. Away from anyone who knew anything about me.

"I promise I will do everything possible to protect you."

"I don't see how you can make such a promise."

"I promise because I know the law. I know how jerks like him think." He placed his hands on my shoulders and pressed his forehead against mine. I closed my eyes, breathing in the sweet smell of the haven he personified.

"Now, let's get some pictures before that ice heals you too fast. Then you can start telling me every detail from the time you stabbed him until you walked into my bar."

Jackson took several pictures of my face while I described my journey, complete with smashing the cell phone after calling the taxi, the bus, and buying the old Subaru. I told him where I left the SUV. He figured the SUV would be stolen or would eventually be impounded, and Troy would have to pay to get it out. He was impressed with the scheming and attention to detail I'd taken in order to hide my tracks. When he asked me to lift my top up a bit to reveal the bruising at my rib cage, I hesitated. I wanted to trust this man, needed to trust him more than anything, but no matter how nice Jackson was, or how much I knew deep down in my heart he wouldn't hurt me, the tiniest speck of doubt continued to creep up the back of my neck and cloud my mind with fear.

"Just up a little and only your side," Jackson said and gave me a reassuring smile.

I lifted the shirt up, just below my breasts, lowering it immediately after he took the pictures. He took some shots of the imprint of Troy's hand on my wrist too. It was so ugly. I couldn't wait for it to fade, which it actually had, some, but there was still enough of it left to show up in a picture.

"You did great in covering your tracks, Lena. I don't think he'll have an easy time locating you, but just for extra precautions, you should probably dye your hair a different color. I have a friend who can help with that. I'll arrange for her to come here. One more thing," he set the camera down, "what name did you use when you bought the car?"

"Lana Martin. Martin was my mother's maiden name."

He frowned. "Did Troy know that?"

"I don't think so. He knew mine was Benton, but we never discussed families. I guess that was one of my mistakes. Maybe if I'd found out more about his family, I would have realized he had the potential for violence. I later found out that his father was in and out of jail for most of Troy's childhood."

"Don't beat yourself up about that one. Not all perpetrators had criminals for parents, and not all victims become perps. For now, go ahead and relax back on the sofa again. I'll get you some more ice, and you can try to sleep while I send these pictures to Luke so he can start the ball rolling on the restraining order."

I slowly sank against the back of the daybed, and waited for him to bring me the ice. I wasn't tired anymore, and I didn't want to be alone. I was scared. I didn't want to be a burden, but for some reason I felt safer with Jackson around. I guess I was beginning to trust him. "Jackson, I don't think I could sleep right at the moment. Do you have any tea or coffee?"

"Oh, of course. Sorry, I got so caught up in helping you, I didn't think about what you might need or want. Which is sort of confusing when you think about it. Are you hungry? I'll make you a sandwich. What kind of sandwich would you like? What kind of tea do you want? I think I have some of that Chamomile tea women like, or would you rather have just plain old

Lipton tea or coffee?"

"You're rambling, but it's sweet. The coffee sounds great, and I'll have a sandwich if you'll join me. Any kind will be fine."

"Yeah, be back in a flash. I'll start the upload of the pictures while I wait for the coffee to brew..." he stopped, turned toward me, pulled his hand through his hair. "Actually, this is really ridiculous."

"What?"

"Me running up and down these stairs, cooking down there and bringing stuff up here. How about if you just come down there and rest? My sofa's much more comfortable than that old daybed anyway, and we have a spare bedroom you can stay in at night. That way I can keep an eye on you while I upload these pictures and start the necessary paperwork for everything."

Chapter 19

Jackson

couldn't believe what I was suggesting, bringing a strange woman into my home. Brodie's home. That was another issue I'd need to deal with before the afternoon was over. It was one thing having her up here, but Brodie might not like the idea of having her down in the same house, even though Lena didn't strike me as a thief or anything. Besides, she could barely walk, let alone steal anything.

She didn't move to get up, just stared at me as if I just appeared out of nowhere.

"Trust me. It will be alright."

"I don't want to be a burden."

"Lena, you're not a burden, and there's something

else you don't know about me."

"What's that?"

"I have a soft spot for injured creatures, and you are injured. I can't help myself, and there's nothing you can say or do to keep me from helping you right now, so you'll just have to give yourself over to me." As I said those last words, her eyes grew huge, and I realized the significance they held. I wished I could take them back. "I'm sorry, that didn't come out right."

"Hope not. One tyrant in my life at a time."

"Good thing for you I'm not into oppression. So, now that that's settled, let's go down to my house. It will be easier on me." Easier and safer, I thought. I could keep a better eye on her, and at least the main house had a security system. I wasn't sure how intelligent this jerk of a husband of hers was, but I didn't want to take any chances.

She didn't move, just continued to stare at me. I held out my hand. "There's a security system down at the house. You'll be safer there." I decided to throw that in to help convince her. "Come on, come down, see if you feel comfortable; if not, you can come back up here tonight if you want. Just come down for now."

Chapter 20

Lena

Reluctantly, I agreed to go down to the main house. I figured being around people might be good for me. God knows I'd been deprived of that privilege long enough. The only people I ever got to see were the clerks at the grocery store or occasionally, the mailman, if I happened to be outside during the mail delivery, but he never left his truck, and only waved from his seat if he happened to notice me.

Jackson helped me down the long stairway leading from the cottage to the house. Once inside he helped make me comfortable on the huge, buttery soft, brown-leather sofa positioned between two dark wooden tables, each sporting the most intricately carved wooden lamps. Across from the sofa stood a tan and light brown stone fireplace sizzling with the scent of burning pine. The two-inch thick slats on the brown shutters of the windows allowed just the right amount of sun in to warm my arms. There was a painting of roaring ocean waves breaking against the side of a steep mountain cliff on the wall behind my head, positioned just a few inches above the sofa. Another picture with scenes of pastoral fields hung above a very old looking cabinet with two doors made of metal slates framed with wood casings. Each door had a series of tiny nail holes making some sort of intricate design. As I looked closer, I realized there was a date etched in the middle of the design: 1861. Jackson must have noticed me staring at the large, beautiful piece of furniture.

"It's an antique pie safe. It belonged to my mom's grandmother. That's where they stored their pies to keep them fresh and safe from critters and bugs. The design on the doors is from the Freemasons society, the fraternal religious organization dating back several centuries. The compass, the square and the trowel are supposed to represent a moral lesson or something. I'm guessing maybe it was something my great grandfather was involved in. To me, it's just a nice piece of furniture. Since I don't bake many pies, it's where I keep my music sheets and some other odds and ends that I have no idea where to put."

He smiled, and I smiled back. I'd heard of the

freemasons, though I didn't know much about them. I was grateful for the history lesson, brief as it was. "Maybe I could bake you one someday as a thank you."

"You have a deal," he said with raised eyebrows. I settled back against the sofa and studied the rest of the room. On the opposite wall hung photographs of people, most likely Jackson's parents and his aunt and uncle among other relatives. Some very old timey photos that might have been pictures of the great grandfather he'd mentioned. A few pictures of Brodie and Jackson were mixed in. It seemed strange to me that guys their age would have so many family pictures on the wall. Maybe it was just something left from their aunt and uncle since this had been their house. My question was answered almost as if Jackson had read my mind.

"The family display of pictures belonged to my aunt. Brodie didn't have the heart to remove them since those are all the people she loved. He said it gave the place a personality and some history. Underneath the macho exterior, my little brother does have a bit of a soft side, though don't tell him I said that."

"No worries," I said. Other than the family pictures, the whole room screamed of masculinity. Glancing through the doorway, I spied the corner of a pool table. This was a house begging for excitement and perfect for social entertaining. I wondered if they did much of that.

Jackson retreated to the kitchen, and I heard the refrigerator open along with the sounds of him placing things on the counter. I felt so helpless and wished I had the strength to give him a hand. My side still ached too much to stand for more than a few minutes. As I rested on the sofa, I considered this man bent on rescuing me. What made him tick? Jackson was a strong name. He was incredibly handsome. I loved the way his hair fell to the bottom of his neck. He hadn't shaved in a couple of days, and the dark stubble made him look a little older. His lips were thick and tender looking. And God, he smelled delicious, something that caught my senses more than once. I wished I had met him under different circumstances, and I suddenly wished I looked and felt better. How could I be attracted to a man so soon after another had treated me so badly?

He came back in carrying a tray with two glasses of milk, a couple of sandwiches and two cups of coffee on it. I had a ton of questions I wanted to ask him, and couldn't help myself as the first one poured out of my mouth as though it couldn't wait to ruin the perfect relationship.

"Jackson, have you ever been married?"

He turned, his face showing surprise at the question. "No."

"Girlfriend?"

"No. Not at the moment." He chuckled softly. "Why do you ask?"

"Well, you're a very attractive guy. I would think girls would be knocking down your door to have you on their arm. Plus, I wanted to make sure I wasn't intruding on anyone. If you did have a girlfriend, I'd hate to have her think the worst."

"Well, any girlfriend of mine would just have to accept the part of me that likes to protect the innocent."

I thought about that, and wondered if he would indeed be helping me if he did have a girlfriend. In some way or another, I bet he would.

"Protecting the innocent and rescuing the wounded is what I do, remember?"

"Yeah. I remember. Jackson …" I hesitated, so many thoughts were running rampant in my head, and I didn't want him to think I was prying. "You said you graduated from college, and then went on to became a cop, then a private investigator." I wanted to be delicate here because he seemed so much younger than someone who could have achieved so much already in life. "I mean, you don't really look old enough to have done all that."

Jackson set the coffee and sandwiches down on the table in front of the sofa and laughed. "Thanks for that. If you wanted to know how old I was you could have just asked."

"Sorry. I'm not used to being so open with anyone. Okay, then how old are you?"

"I'll be twenty-three in a couple of months." When I simply stared at him and frowned, he added, "I graduated high school at sixteen, and went directly into Berkeley. I did my four years in pre-law, but always kept music as a minor. I guess you might say I was an over-achiever back then." He sat down on the sofa beside me and handed me a plate with a sandwich on it.

"Thanks," I said. "It looks good."

Without looking at me, he asked, "Uh ... how long were you married to him?"

"A little less than a year ... it was stupid to marry him. I only knew him a few weeks. He was a bit over-protective, but never did anything that made me think he would hurt me until after we were married. Aside from that night after dancing with Weezer, which, at the time, I'd figured I'd deserved, that first couple of weeks was O.K, at least until the episode when he hit me during dinner. Everything *was* wonderful." I took a bite of the sandwich, chewed, and swallowed, "Mmmm ... turkey. It's funny, you know, I never thought of myself as being weak, but now, I don't know what I am. I planned to leave him after the first time. I just needed to find a way out, but as time progressed, it seemed to get harder and harder. He kept tabs on everything I did and everywhere I went. Escape seemed impossible."

"You don't have to be weak to be manipulated. It seems to me he was the weak one. It takes a weak man to threaten and hurt the ones he is supposed to love and protect. You, sweetheart, were brave and strong. Brave to endure, and strong to get out."

Chapter 21

Jackson

I left Lena in the living room with a small fire in the fireplace so she'd stay warm, and went to send Luke the pictures and other information he'd need to start the process for a restraining order and divorce. When I came back to the living room, I found Lena asleep.

I let her sleep for a couple of hours, and once the sun slipped down below the horizon, it seemed a bit chilly. I relit the fire and pulled a blanket up over her being careful not to disturb her, but she stirred and opened her eyes.

"Oh hey, I thought you were sleeping."

"I was, but I've also been thinking."

"About?"

"This might seem silly, but I feel so helpless. I mean, not just because I'm hurt, but here you've taken me in, a complete stranger, and I have no way of repaying you. Maybe you could let me work in your pub when I'm feeling better? I don't know, washing glasses or something. I don't have much experience— well any, actually—as a waitress or anything, but I'm not used to having someone care for me, and it's just sort of weird since you hardly know me."

I knelt in front of her and took her hands in mine. "I know enough about you to know you're a decent person, that you've been wronged, and that you need help. That's all I need to know." I smiled at her.

"What?"

"The swelling on your eye seems to have gone down almost completely, it looks as if all the ice worked."

I smiled and stroked my hand lightly down the side of her cheek, and again wished I could make her bruises go away with a brush of my fingers so I could revel in the taste of her full, generous lips. *No, Jackson, not this woman.* As much as I wanted her, it would have to be on her terms, when she was ready.

"When your bruises are healed, and when you're feeling back to normal completely, would you be open to some self defense training?"

"I guess so."

"Great. Until then, concentrate on getting stronger.

I'm not worried about you paying me back for anything. If I didn't want you here, you wouldn't be."

The front door slammed, and Rufus howled as Lena's body jerked, and Rosie scurried under the sofa.

"Jackson, here's your guitar. You left it at the bar again. Quiet Rufus." Brodie blew into the room carrying two guitars over his shoulder.

"Brodie, do you have to announce your presence by slamming the door?" I let go of Lena's hands, got up, and took the guitars from my brother.

"You know me, bro, I like to make a grand entrance. Oh, hey, Lana, how's your eye?"

"It's Lena, by the way," I told him.

"Huh?"

"It's Lena, not Lana. Who's got the bar?"

"I thought you said ... Derrick. Sorry." He glanced toward Lena, "I thought you said Lana the other day."

I decided to let it go, no point in explaining. "Derrick, good, is he closing or are you going back?"

"I'm going back, I'm starving. Have you guys eaten dinner yet? Want to order Chinese?"

I looked at Lena—she nodded. "Yeah, sure. You order. Any particular item you like best, Lena?"

"Sesame beef, spicy."

I raised my brow and smiled at Brodie.

"Now there's a girl after my own heart," Brodie chimed. "Spicy it is."

When Brodie and I were alone in the kitchen, he startled me with, "What's with the name switch?"

"She lied," I answered, not thinking too much

about it.

"She lied?"

"She was being cautious. Give her a break. Listen, Brodie, she's going to stay here in the guestroom instead of the cottage."

"Wait. She lies about her name, and you decide it's okay to open up my house to her?"

"She was scared shitless. You'd lie too under the right circumstances."

"I see. Why don't you just pass over all the preliminaries and let her stay in your room?"

"Don't be snide, Brodie."

"Snide? It wasn't meant to be snide, Jack, just stating the obvious."

"What's that supposed to mean?"

"Come on Jackson, you know you're falling head over heels for her. It hasn't even been a week since she walked into the bar, and you're tripping over your own feet just to make her comfortable. You were supposed to put her up in the cottage, now she's in the guestroom. What the hell is it with you and the injured?"

"What's your problem, Brodie? And what the hell is it with you and all the women you bring home all the time? Fucking a different one every night isn't going to make her come back. I get it. You loved her; she broke your heart, but not every woman is like Beth." I knew that hurt, bringing up the girl who'd broken his heart, possibly scarred him for life it seemed by the way he was acting, but jeez, he needed to back off.

"Maybe not!" he yelled. "Maybe not, but at least I'm dealing with it, and we aren't talking about her or me."

"That's how you deal? By not caring? Are you saying I shouldn't care—that I shouldn't want to help someone in need?"

"No. I'm just saying open your eyes, brother. I don't have a problem with you wanting to rescue the unfortunate—just don't kid yourself on this one. You already care too much. I see it—I saw it when I came home, the way you were looking at her, holding her hands." Brodie scowled and shoved past me. "Where's the phone?"

I handed him the portable, and he ordered dinner.

Chapter 22

Lena

he next day Jackson had his friend, Leslie, from the Hair Affair come by the house to change my hair color. He'd explained a little about my situation, but only gave the necessary details. When he told her I needed some clothes, she'd offered to get some. He had me talk to her on the phone first so I could give her my sizes, and she arrived with a pair of jeans, a black pullover top and some underwear. They were all brand new from what I could tell, especially since they still had the tags on them. She explained that her shop was located right next door to a women's boutique downtown. After she changed my hair color and gave me a trim, I changed into the clothes she brought, then sat back down for the final touches she wanted to make with my hair. As she brushed and blew the new light strands dry, I stared at the girl in the mirror hardly recognizing her. Leslie bleached my dark auburn hair to a pretty shade of light gold that I thought made my skin look pale.

When I walked out of the kitchen where Leslie had performed her magic transformation, Jackson was sitting on the sofa playing his guitar. He looked up from his chords, took a double take, and smiled.

"Hey, I thought you were beautiful as a redhead, but now you're a golden haired angel."

"You like?"

He leaned the guitar against the side of the sofa and approached me. Standing very close to me, his knuckles grazed my cheeks as he pulled several strands through his long fingers. I swallowed the stone forming in my throat. With his face mere inches from mine, his eyes roamed my face, and then he nodded slowly. My stomach knotted for a moment before he spoke. "Yeah. Did you have light hair when you were a kid?" Was that admiration in his eyes? I quickly glanced at the floor, not wanting him to know that his expression confused me, and took a step backwards.

"Yeah, I guess. Maybe more of a strawberry color. It turned dark red when I was still very young, though.

"I like." Jackson wiggled his eyebrows. I couldn't help laughing when I remembered that this man standing here before me was not Troy. And I had to keep reminding myself that this man was nothing like

Troy.

"Here." He handed me a package. "I bought you something." I reached in the bag and pulled out a pair of thick rimmed black glasses with fake diamond studs on the sides." He stood back, studied me. "Even if that slime does hunt you down, he won't be looking for a blonde haired vixen with glasses. Now you can come out to the pub with me." He kept his eyes on me as he said, "Leslie, you did an awesome job."

"Thanks, Jackson. That'll be forty dollars."

"Only forty? What about the clothes?" he asked.

"The forty is for the clothes. The hair is on me."

"Thanks, Leslie." He handed her a hundred dollar bill and said, "Keep the change. Remember, you never did this, and you never met Lana before. Right?" My eyes flicked to his, and I smiled at his use of the fake name.

"Your secret's safe with me." She turned to Lena. "Honey, I don't know who or what you're running from, but I know you'll be safe here with Jackson. His uncle used to come see me once a month for a haircut. The man couldn't keep from bragging enough about his nephews. Brodie and Jackson are the two best guys you'll ever meet."

"Thank you very much. I'm beginning to believe that."

"Well, you keep on believing it, honey because it's the truth. You take care, and don't forget, you'll need a touch up in about six weeks if you want to keep that pretty, golden color looking natural. If you play and sing as well as Jack says, I'm sure I'll be seeing you in the pub sooner than that though."

Chapter 23

Jackson

The late afternoon sun filtered through the window shining right in Lena's eyes, and making her squint from where she sat on the sofa. I got up and closed the drapes, which made the room dark, so I flipped the switch on the lamp beside me. I sat in the old easy chair that my uncle spent many nights in, blowing on his harmonica. Uncle Joe once played and sang in a band when he was my age, and from what I'd heard by the awesome sounds he'd produced just sitting in that chair, he was pretty good. He'd been my musical inspiration, and I thought of him as I strummed out a new tune on my guitar that had been floating around in my head for several days. The words were coming together, and as I jotted them down, rearranged the flow, their meaning hit me like a crate full of bricks. I was writing a song about Lena. Like the fawn I'd nursed back to health when I was a kid. A song about a broken spirit on its way to healing, I hoped.

Brodie had been right, of course. I had wanted Lena from the moment I first set eyes on her. I knew when I watched her walk in the bar she was beautiful, even with her black eye. She was a beautifully wounded and broken soul that I couldn't turn my back on. I had been instantly drawn to her as her bruised, damaged body limped from the door to one of the stools at the bar.

Lena spent the days lounging on our sofa, and nights in the spare bedroom with the door locked. Though she never said anything about locking the door, I heard the click each night when she shut the door. I couldn't blame her, not after what she'd gone through. I let Rufus stay with her at night to give her a sense of protection. Not that Rufus would or could protect her— he was just a lovable lump of pure unconditional love mostly. Well, at least he'd keep her feet warm while she slept, I mused. It'd been hell every night, knowing she was sleeping right in the next room. However wrong it was to want her, I couldn't shake the feeling. I knew it would have to be her decision though. If there was ever going to be something between us, she would have to initiate it. I could wait. If she even wanted me.

Lena was healing and gaining her strength back. I

figured she was still pretty sore, but she smiled a little more often. I'd gone out and purchased some more clothes for her. I bought three pairs of jeans and about seven tops. I also bought her a pair of running shoes and some workout clothes, as well as a baseball cap. I told her, once she was well enough, in addition to self-defense training she had to start going out with me on my daily run.

By the end of the first week, the swelling in her eye had subsided, and the black and blue hues surrounding it turned a greenish yellow tint. Though I didn't know firsthand, she told me the bruising on her side also showed signs of healing and had turned to the same light color.

I heard Lena sigh from where she stretched out on the sofa, and I glanced up. She looked bored silly. I turned over the paper I'd been scribbling notes and lyrics on, and went to fetch my spare guitar. I handed the wooden six-string to her and sat beside her.

"Do you know this one?" I asked, strumming a tune.

"No, teach it to me."

"Okay, listen."

She listened then strummed, mimicking my fingers.

"You're quick," I said.

I played some more, and she copied each note immediately after me. I nodded. "That's it. Let's start at the beginning." We strummed the tune as if we'd been playing together for years. When the song finished she laughed, the sound of her laughter filled the room with warmth. "That was fun," I said.

I played a few notes of the song I'd been toying with, and she quickly picked up the tune and followed along. She was good. "What is that?" she asked. It's really pretty."

"Thanks. Just something I've been playing around with in my head."

"Well, it's beautiful. I hope you finish it."

"Does it have any lyrics?"

"I'm working on them. Come on, let's run through that other one again."

We played a few more tunes that she knew until she stopped and grinned. "Oh, I've missed this. Troy smashed my guitar into pieces early on in our marriage. He came home one evening when I'd been working on a new song, trying to work out the kinks you know. Anyway, dinner was on the stove simmering." She'd hardly touched the wine I poured for her, but picked it up and took a small sip, placing it back down before repositioning her fingers along the strings. "He'd come in complaining about something at work and wanted to know why his dinner wasn't on the table. At that moment, I realized I should get up and see to it, and when I put my guitar down, he picked it up and smashed it against the wall. He said his dinner should have been my first priority when he came home. He expected me to be attending to him, not sitting around playing with toys, so he smashed my guitar. He said next time it would be my face."

I cupped her chin in my palm. She must have felt self-conscience at the gesture and flinched.

"Sorry." I lowered my hand.

She looked down at the guitar and gently splayed her fingers across the frets. Picking up the glass of wine with her other, she took a quick sip then frowned. "I think I need some water." She leaned the guitar against the side of the sofa and stood.

I stood as well and tenderly took her arm at the elbow, stopping her from leaving. She turned and looked up at me, bewilderment evident in her eyes. She was close to me, our chests nearly touching. "I'm sorry he treated you so badly," I whispered—my lips just a couple of inches from hers.

Apprehensive, I searched her blue eyes, looking for a clue, a hint as to what she might be feeling. How would she react to my touch? The last thing I wanted was to stir up memories of unwanted dirty sex.

Chapter 24

Lena

I hesitated, not sure what to do. Jackson stood too close to me, his voice just a whisper next to my ear, and maybe sort of sexy. I wasn't sure what sexy sounded like, and I wasn't sure why I even had that thought. I wasn't feeling sexy. I still felt ugly, and I wasn't used to the tenderness. My eye was healing and not completely black and blue anymore. More greenish now, but makeup didn't cover much, so I'm sure I looked very plain and unattractive. My heart pounded in my chest as he stared into my eyes. I couldn't move, or didn't want to move. Afraid to breathe, I stood still, not wanting the moment to end. I didn't want him to think I wanted him that way. I didn't want him to think I didn't want him that way. My mind became a jumble of confusion. I did want him I thought. I wanted to be in his arms, to feel his lips on mine. I wanted to know if they were as soft as they looked. I wanted to know if he would taste sweet like the red wine we were drinking. I wanted his touch on my skin, to feel his fingers graze up my arm, but I wasn't sure if I was ready for that intimacy. As though he could sense my thoughts, he ran his thumb down my forearm and turned my hand over. Taking my hand into his, he seemed to study the lines in my palm. His thumb made little circles over them, and his eyes flicked to mine. "It's okay," he said. Though I didn't know what he meant. I swallowed hard, wondering what was about to happen. Then, all of a sudden, Troy's scary and dangerous eyes flooded my mind. My splayed hand looked dwarfed against Jackson's broad chest as I shoved him out of my way and ran from the room.

I stood in the kitchen for a moment, not understanding why I was even there. I glanced around at the gold and black speckled granite counter, searching for a reason. The opened bottle of wine we'd been drinking stood right next to a little picture frame holding a photo of Jackson and Brodie, and another man I guessed might be their uncle. The family resemblance was strong. It might have been their father. Jackson never told me what happened to his parents. He and Brodie didn't appear to be much younger than they were now in the snapshot, the scene around them festively adorned with a Christmas tree behind them and other decorations; their arms casually draped around each other as they all stood grinning at whoever snapped the picture. They looked so ... normal. I sucked in the sob that wanted so badly to escape, and took a deep breath. Not like Troy.

Jackson was not Troy.

Jackson was not Troy.

I silently repeated that simple little sentence several times as I breathed in slowly through my nose, out through my mouth, praying Jackson wouldn't come in and find me so unhinged.

I managed to pull myself back together just as Jackson entered the kitchen, and the horror on his face almost undid me again. No, not horror ... pity. He pitied me, and that made me sick to my stomach. Only needy people were pitied, and I never wanted to be placed in that category.

"Are you okay?" Jackson asked, standing inside the doorjamb, acting reluctant about entering his own kitchen. God, I hated myself right then.

I managed a nod and stood, wringing my hands in front of me. I didn't know what to do with them. "I'm sorry, I don't know why I let him into my head. The way I keep talking about him, you'd think ..." my words trailed off. I didn't know how I wanted to finish that sentence. I had talked so casually about Troy, like he was a long lost friend or something, and that couldn't have been further from the truth. My desire for

Jackson really had me confused. I glanced toward the sink, finally remembering the water I'd originally come into the kitchen for.

Chapter 25

Lena

I stayed inside the kitchen doorway, not wanting to invade her space, but wanting her to know I was there. She seemed so fragile, yet so determined to overcome whatever demons continued to possess her. Troy demons I supposed. I wanted to bang my own head against the wall. I blamed myself for making her act so injured, so vulnerable, yet I knew it hadn't been me that made her that way. It had been dickwad, Troy. If he ever came within twenty-feet of her again, I knew I'd be in trouble. I didn't think I'd be able to stop myself from bashing his head in, which was a rather insane thought, considering I was not a violent person. Would I ever be able to break down the walls of the prison he'd trapped her in? I'd gotten too close. I knew it when I whispered in her ear, but I wanted to be close. I wanted her to be comfortable with me. To realize she could feel safe with me.

"No. It's my fault. I never meant to crowd you that way or make you feel uncomfortable. Believe me." I took a cautious step toward her, but stopped as her left foot went behind her as though she were afraid of me. "I only want you to feel safe around here. I would never hurt you." I took another step toward her, and she didn't move. When I got close enough, I held out my hand to her. I hoped the smile on my face came across as warm and reassuring as I meant for it to. I guess I succeeded when she slowly extended her hand toward mine. It took a few seconds before our fingertips touched, but once they did, I didn't waste any time and wrapped my fingers around hers. I didn't pull her or make her move, just held her hand, and she smiled at me. Her eyes lit up like sparklers, and my heart sang a sweet song of praise.

As we stood in the kitchen holding hands, I noticed the sun going down. The sunset over the lake was always beautiful this time of day.

"I have an idea," I said, and let the uncontrollable smile grow wide on my face as I tugged her out the kitchen door with me. "Come with me."

"Wait," she protested, but I didn't stop walking as I coaxed her along to the car.

"Where are we going?" she added with a slight

giggle.

"You see that?" I pointed at the sun blaring in the partially clouded sky.

"Yes."

"Well, it's about to make the most beautiful picture you've ever seen, and I know the best spot to watch it from." I held the passenger door open for her and she got in, fastening her seatbelt. I hurried to the other side of the car. "Oh, wait a minute," I yelled, holding my hand up as I ran back inside and grabbed the bottle of wine off the counter. I found two red, plastic cups in the cupboard, and ran back to the car. With my free hand, I dug in the front pocket of my jeans for the keys and slipped in behind the wheel. We didn't have much time, so I needed to get moving as quickly as possible, and I fishtailed the back end of the car a bit on the way out of the gravel driveway. Lena gasped as her body swerved toward mine and her hand landed on my thigh. She quickly removed it, and I glanced at her. "Sorry, about that. Are you okay?" She nodded, keeping her eyes forward as though she might be able to help me control the car if she did. "Don't worry. I'll be careful." I stole a glance at her determined face and shot her a grin as she nibbled on her bottom lip. I almost wished she'd left her hand there. No, not almost.

Chapter 26
Lena

The tires scrunched along the gravel mixed in with dirt until we made it onto the paved road. I don't know what got into Jackson, but all of a sudden, he seemed like a little kid eager to show me his new prized possession, and he managed to instantly draw my mind out of the fearscape I'd drummed up. I worried a bit when my hand fell onto his lap as we swerved coming out of the driveway, but he didn't make a big deal about it. It embarrassed me some. It was an accident, and I didn't want him to get the wrong idea. Not that I didn't like him, I did. I wished I could have just left my hand on Jackson's firm thigh. I blinked my eyes, willing the pleasurable moment away. I couldn't allow my thoughts to go there right now, so … so soon after what just happened with Troy.

Jackson turned the SUV down something resembling a road, but from the looks of all the brush and trees growing amongst and through it, I couldn't be sure it was an actual road.

"Don't worry," he said as I braced my hand at the top of the glove box for support. "I know this road like the back of my hand."

Road? What road? I wanted to ask, but decided my energy was better spent looking out for unsuspecting animals we might crash into, or worse yet, a cliff side that would take us plummeting to our deaths. I didn't dare take my eyes off the path for fear I might miss the attack of a tree right before we rammed into it, killing us both. I wanted to be aware of my last couple seconds of life. When he stopped the car beside a large oak tree and placed the gearshift into park, I breathed out a sigh of relief.

He heard me and laughed. "Did that ride scare you?"

"Maybe just a little," I admitted, releasing my fingers from their death grip on the dash. "Where are we?"

"Come on," he said without answering me. He came over to my side of the SUV and opened my door. With the wine bottle and cups in his other hand, he waved them in front of himself, bending a little at the waist he bowed his head and splayed his other hand and arm out toward the forest. "This way, m'lady."

I smiled and stepped out, taking the outstretched hand that he offered to me.

Glancing around the woodsy surroundings, I couldn't imagine where he was taking me. The little voice inside my head wanted to scream, *No! Don't go into the woods*, but I managed to squash down the panic rising in my chest. If Jackson wanted to hurt me he would have done it by now. I took a deep breath and followed him into the forest. The narrow path we entered didn't look too bad, growing wider as we continued, and resembling more of a trail than it did in the beginning. A small hill sloped up toward our right with pine trees looming from the ground as we kept going. Some were so tall I wondered how they stayed straight, growing from the side of the slope that way. To our left, the hillside swept downward with trees covering almost every inch of free space.

"Let's hurry. It's getting close to sunset." Jackson said as he led the way, pulling my hand with him. My side still tender, I clutched at it with my free hand. Jackson noticed and slowed down. "We're almost there. Stay close." I kept my eyes on the ground watching where Jackson stepped, making sure to step right behind him.

When we stopped walking, I looked up. My eyes widened at the sight of the huge expanse of water in front of us. "Over here." Jackson tugged to our left and led me over to a small metal motorboat perched upside down on the bank, secured to a tree with heavy twine. He untied it and turned it over. Under it, two oars lie side by side. "It's not fancy or anything, but this is my fishing boat, and this," he gestured toward the water, "is my fishing hole. And in about ten minutes, that sun is going to sink just below the water's edge over that way. His eyes were bright with excitement as he pointed down at the far end of the lake. "If we hurry, we can catch it. Take that end," he said, motioning to the opposite end of the boat from the motor end he was now lifting. I helped him pick up the boat, and we carried it to the water. It wasn't as heavy as I had thought it would be. "Hop in." I did as he told me and immediately sat down at the end away from the motor. Jackson pushed the boat away from the shore and hopped in.

I sat staring at Jackson. He wore a silly grin that he didn't seem to realize until he glanced at me and frowned. "You might want to turn around and face that way."

"Okay," I picked up my legs and twirled around to face the front of the boat. He started the engine, which was to my surprise, relatively quiet, and we floated away from the beach toward the sinking sun.

It was the most beautiful picture I'd ever seen. The colors of blood-red orange mingled with purple covered the entire sky as wisps of clouds scattered throughout. The way the reddish-orange met the ocean looked as if the sky just above the water was on fire. I couldn't contain the gasp that escaped my lips. "Oh my God,

Jackson, this is beautiful."

"I thought you'd like it."

"Like it? I love it." I turned briefly to see his grin, or just to make sure he was there and real. I wanted to reach out and touch him just to make sure I wasn't in some beautiful dream that I'd wake up from, disappointed that I couldn't stay asleep. He sat straight; confident looking with his hand on the steering shaft of the motor. My God, he was so handsome. His green eyes shimmered with the light cast from the sinking sun, and he smiled at me. Satisfied he was real and I wasn't dreaming I quickly swiveled back around. I didn't want to miss a single moment of the majestic sensation before my eyes, consuming every inch of my soul. "This truly has to be heaven," I whispered, knowing, as real as this beautiful moment was, it could only be temporary.

Chapter 27

Jackson

As Lena whispered those words, my heart sank two inches in my chest and ached for the young woman before me. I don't think I'd ever heard or seen such a beautiful statement in regards to my favorite spot on earth. Of course, I'd never brought anyone here before, other than Brodie. Actually, Brodie and I discovered this fishing hole together when we were kids. The special part about this stretch of the river was the stillness of the water. The only rippling was the small wake the boat made, and when I turned off the engine, the tranquil water looked like glass. A soft, but warm early spring breeze caught a few strands of Lena's beautiful new blonde tendrils.

They pressed against her cheek into her lips, and she brushed them away as she turned to glance back at me with a wide grin. The moment the magic of the beauty surrounded her, she was like a sponge, absorbing every molecule of wonderful energy the sunset provided. It was a gorgeous one too. I was grateful that I was able to show it to her.

"Yes, it is beautiful," I finally managed to say, after being so swept up in her reaction. I cut the engine and reached for the bottle of wine. Pouring a little into each cup, I made my way to the spot on the bench next to her and handed her one. "The beauty of this place is what keeps me coming back. I don't really care about fishing so much, though on a hot summer day, with a few beers, I've been known to disappear here for several hours. The best time of the day is right now." She sipped the wine and kept her eyes on the sunset, while I couldn't tear my own eyes away from her profile. "I'll have to bring you here on the fourth of July. The fireworks they light off each year are spectacular and reflect off the water as they illuminate the sky."

She glanced at me and caught me staring, but all I could do was smile. She averted her eyes though, and mumbled, "I don't know if I'll still be here in the summer."

The statement took me completely off guard. "What? Why not?"

She gave a slight uncertain shake of her head, but

didn't answer. I had to remind myself that this girl, as beautiful as she was—and as much as I wanted her—didn't belong to me.

"I can't stay here, Jackson. You've been terrific, a wonderful friend, more than I could have ever hoped for, but if I remain in one place for too long, I'm afraid he'll find me. In fact, I'm certain of it."

"You don't know that. We'll have a restraining order issued against him. I won't let him harm you ever again, I promise."

"You can't make that promise. How could you? Troy isn't the type of person to pay attention to a restraining order. I know he's searching for me right now."

"From what you told me, you've done a very good job of covering your tracks. Why would he even think of you being here?"

"I don't know. But if there is a way, he will find it."

"Jackson, people are starting to ask about you. The band wants to know when you're going to join us again, and customers keep asking for you." Brodie held the kitchen screen door wide open, letting Rufus in. The dog came barreling through the opening so fast he skidded across the hardwood floor, stopping just short of the stainless steel refrigerator, but not soon enough that his wet nose didn't make smudge marks across the middle of it.

"Tell them I'll be there soon. Jeez, can't a guy take a little vaca?" I hadn't been going into the pub as much as I normally did. I didn't want to leave Lena alone. But after the first week, she insisted I go in, said that she would be fine at the house by herself. I agreed, but I only managed to stay for an hour. Once I walked into the bar, I started worrying so much I couldn't concentrate, and took off for home shortly afterwards. Since then, I hadn't tried going in again.

"Vacation? Look, I don't need you to help at the bar, and you can take all day, every day, doing whatever it is you want, but the band is suffering because you're putting some stranger ahead of your obligations to them. We are good, but we need our lead guitarist and singer. If you don't show up soon, I heard the other guys talking about finding someone to take your place."

"They can't do that. It's my band, my place."

"Our band, and well, they recognized the fact that we're losing customers too."

"Don't you have any compassion?"

"Yeah, I have compassion, but Jack, you've become obsessed with this girl. I just don't get you. You've put your entire life on hold for a complete stranger, and on top of that, instead of having her stay up in the cottage like she was supposed to, she's moved in here with us. Why is that Jack? Why do you have such a hard on for this girl, why are you so hell-bent on rescuing every fucked up, damaged soul in this

163

universe, and why did my house suddenly become a refuge for them?"

"Stop being an ass, Brodie."

"I will, as soon as you stop being a sap." Just as the words left Brodie's mouth, I looked up to see Lena standing in the doorway to the kitchen. By the somber look on her face, I knew she'd heard every word of the fucked up conversation that Brodie and I just had.

"Lena, wait!" I called out as she hurried away toward the guest room. "Way to go, jerkwad," I muttered to Brodie as I pushed my way past him. I caught the guest room door just before she had the chance to shut and lock it. "Listen, Lena, don't pay any attention to Brodie. He's … he's just looking out for the bar. He didn't mean anything by what he said."

"Brodie's right. I shouldn't be staying down here. I should have stayed upstairs like the original arrangement. It's probably best if I leave in the morning."

"Leave? You mean go back upstairs to the cottage?"

"No, I mean leave all together. I should get moving anyway, the sooner the better."

"No. Please don't. Look, I know you want to pay your way. I completely understand that. I want you to feel comfortable. Maybe you can put in a few hours at the bar?"

"Doing what, Jack? I don't have any experience."

"Hell, it doesn't take much experience to wash glasses and wipe off tables, maybe even carry a few drinks out to the customers sitting at them. At least if you're there, I know you're safe. And I'm sure the band would love for you to do a couple numbers with us. I know I would."

Chapter 28

Lena

I locked the door to the room and sank down on the floor. My face fell into my hands, and I couldn't help the tears that flowed beneath them. My only relief—I managed to hold them back while talking to Jackson. I didn't want him to know I'd been affected so much. What Brodie said had hurt, but I really couldn't blame him. This was Brodie's house, and I had to admit, he didn't have the same bond with me that I had with Jackson. A connection I worried over. A connection I would have welcomed a couple of years ago. I appreciated everything he was doing for me. I only wished I could return the affection that he seemed to have for me.

Jackson wanted more, more than I could—or was ready to—give. I knew by the way his green eyes, so full of compassion and concern, drank in my every movement, by the way he spent all of his free time with me, and the way he always managed to stand so close to me whenever he had the opportunity. I knew by the way he'd sometimes let his hand brush against mine when he thought I might not notice. I noticed.

I glanced around the small room. The dark mahogany dresser with a feminine lace doily and white lace curtains in the window suggested that Brodie and Jack hadn't redecorated this room since they moved in, and instead had left it pretty much the way their aunt must have had it. The bedspread, or I guess it was more of a quilt made up of delicate little squares of assorted pastels flowing together in a sort of ocean wave pattern, gave the room an old-fashioned flavor. It was a nice room, but it wasn't mine.

The more I studied the room, the more I wanted to move back upstairs and start doing some of my own decorating. I stood, went to the window and looked up at the cottage. Excitement grew inside me with the prospect of decorating a home without Troy giving me grief about every little item. He was always so opinionated about those things. You'd think he'd actually possessed some sense of design, but I'm sure he just didn't want me to have anything pretty. He would only allow pictures and other decorations he'd picked out. The only thing in our house that had any hint of me in it was that damn picture hanging on the wall by the stairs of the two of us. I'd learned early on in the marriage not to bother buying anything. Troy would only take it back to the store, or if it wasn't too expensive, smash it in a fit of anger. He once threw a heart-shaped paperweight at me. It hit me in the shoulder and made a bruise that lasted two weeks. I hope the frame he knocked off the wall above the stairs shattered into a million pieces, and that the glass tore the picture to shreds.

The next day, I packed up the few clothes I'd accumulated over the past week and carried them up the steps to the cottage. Jackson, Rufus, and Rosie followed close on my heels. I had to smile; a trio of new best friends.

Jackson stepped in and placed a full bag of groceries on the counter in the kitchen, insisting that I'd need everything in there, and that they were only some basic items to get me started like coffee, butter and bread. "You should probably make a list of things you want or need, and when I go to the store I'll pick them up for you."

"That's really kind of you, but you know, I can do my own shopping. Besides, now that I'm not covered with bruises I'd really like to investigate this little town of yours. Maybe do some sightseeing."

"Well, here you go." Jackson handed me the key and stuck his hands in his pockets, taking a couple of steps backward, almost as if he were shy. "It's all yours. You can pay me once a month, starting on the first of the month."

"But today is only the eighteenth. What about this month?"

"I know. Look, Lena. We don't need the money. So, just stay here, make it your home, and start paying on the first."

I swallowed, not sure how to respond to his generosity. I needed a place to stay. I didn't have much money, certainly not enough for a hotel or some other place where the rent would most likely be way over what this place should be. He was already giving me a break on the rent, but to let me stay here for the next couple of weeks for free seemed like too much. But one thing I'd learned over the past few days about Jackson Beaumont was that he didn't take no for an answer when it came to offering his help.

"Thanks, Jack. I'll find a way to repay you."

"We'll see." He glanced up at the dark clouds forming. "Get in there before it starts pouring. I'll bring up some firewood for you. The heater works, but I heard from past tenants that the fireplace works better."

I smiled and headed into the room. It seemed colder inside than it was out. I thought I'd try the heater just to take the chill off while waiting for the firewood. When I turned to ask Jackson how to turn on the heater he'd already gone, so I closed the door.

I found the thermostat for the heater on the wall

next to the bathroom. It seemed fairly simple to figure out. It had a switch under the words heat, cool and off. Another switch stuck out under the words auto and on and was positioned to auto. I left it there and switched the other one to heat. I set the temperature to seventy degrees as warm air flowed out of the vent on the floor and the swirling sound of the fan filled the room. After a few minutes, I had to turn it off. The loud noise from the fan became so annoying I could barely think, and I understood why he went to get the firewood.

Chapter 29

Jackson

After getting Lena all situated upstairs with plenty of firewood to last the night and maybe a little into tomorrow, I reluctantly, and with a great amount of self-control, left her alone. It was one of the most difficult things I'd ever had to do, well, aside from accepting that I had to let that fawn go when I was a kid.

I went to the computer to check emails and noticed that Luke emailed the divorce petition and restraining order over, so I called him to let him know I got them.

"Yeah, Jack, the guy played it really cool when the process server handed him the papers, even seemed shocked and hurt that Lena would divorce him.

Harington told the server he just couldn't understand why she would leave him and file a restraining order against him, considering he'd never laid a hand on her. He told the server that he loved her more than life itself, and would never even dream of hurting her. The guy even managed to get all teary-eyed." Luke chuckled.

"What an ass-wipe," I said.

"Yeah, a real model citizen. I managed to find some more information on him. He was arrested about five years ago for beating a neighbor's dog. They couldn't prove anything since nobody actually saw him do it, so he got off. The neighbor claimed Harrington was always swearing at the dog, and had threatened to beat the holy crap out of it several times. But the charges were dropped after the neighbor admitted he didn't see him do it and just assumed he had."

"Too bad they couldn't pin it on him."

"Yeah, but just having the accusations on record helps your friend's case. I'm sure if I had the time to dig further I'd come up with some more dirt."

"Thanks, Luke. You've done plenty. So, now we just sit back and wait, right?

"Yeah, then it's smooth sailing. In approximately ninety days, I'll submit the final papers. I'll get the judge to move quickly on this. He's a friend of mine and owes me."

"You're the best, Luke."

"Be careful, Jackson, this guy is sly and dangerous. I don't think a restraining order's going to deter him from trying to take what he thinks belongs to him."

I had no doubt about Luke's warning. But I did have reservations as to whether or not I could talk Lena into sticking around long enough to be here when the papers came for her to sign.

Having her move in upstairs, as much as I wanted to keep her here with me, was a good start though. I knew she was safe, and I knew she'd heal better, both inside and out if given an opportunity to make a new home for herself. Staying in the guest bedroom of a house with two guys didn't give her much opportunity for that.

Only now, I had to think of some way to keep a closer eye on her since she wasn't exactly right by my side all the time. Oh, man, now I sounded like a crazy stalker or something. I was pathetic, and started to make myself sick.

Maybe Brodie was right, and I should back off. Let the woman live her life without me butting in with my two-cents-worth of bullshit. No doubt that's the way she saw it. Unsolicited advice was usually considered boring and annoying. Brodie was right; I couldn't keep treating her as if she were some injured animal like my fawn, but, God, if something happened, if that creep ever found her, I'd never forgive myself for not being there for her. Now I was beginning to annoy even myself. I cared too much. I was in too deep, and I didn't know how to pull myself up and out of the box of emotions I'd created.

Chapter 30

Lena

I awoke with a start. I'd had a dream that Troy called me on my phone telling me he knew where I was. A phone I didn't have anymore. I had to admit; I was very relieved about that. I knew I'd covered my tracks really well, and that he'd have to do some heavy duty investigating to locate me. At this point, though, I didn't want to underestimate the power that I knew he possessed when it came to getting what he wanted.

He was ruthless to the core. I'd witnessed him track down a guy who'd owed him money once. I remember being amazed at his persistence and the extreme measures he'd gone through to locate the guy, who at the time, seemed to have escaped the entire planet, not just the city of Medford. So, I knew if I stayed in one place too long, Troy would eventually find me. I took the dream as an omen, and decided right then, no matter how much I loved it here or how wonderful I thought Jackson was, I needed to make this place just a temporary stop. Jackson was a great guy. A guy I could fall hard for if I let myself. But knowing that Troy would eventually find me, I couldn't risk staying here too much longer. I'd give it a month or two just so I could pay Jackson back for all he'd done for me, and then I'd leave. Maybe continue heading south. The further I distanced myself from Oregon, the better.

When Jackson came up the other day with the divorce papers, I'd almost refused to sign them for fear that if I did, Troy would be able to find me merely through osmosis. I knew no matter what I did, sign them or not, letting the divorce go through wouldn't make Troy stop looking for me. But Jackson seemed to think a divorce would make a world of difference. How could I argue with the nicest guy on the planet, a guy so determined to look out for my best interests? Jackson had been … well, still is my savior.

Over the past few days, I'd stayed inside and just vegged in front of the TV watching reruns of Charmed and Buffy. They'd been my favorite shows as a kid, and brought some comfort with memories of a time when it was just me and my mom. But I got lucky yesterday when I found a marathon of The Walking Dead. Troy hadn't allowed me to watch it. He said it was stupid, and asked why I would want to watch a show about dead people eating people. Watching it now gave me an extra amount of satisfaction in the fact that he couldn't control me anymore. I hadn't seen Jackson at all during the past couple of days, and I wondered if I'd said or did something to make him not come up and see how I was. It was almost as though he'd done a one-eighty. He'd been so worried and helpful before. So… oh, my, God. Did he pull away because he thought that's what I wanted? Or maybe he just found someone else he'd rather give his attention to. I knew it was probably better if he did, but for some reason that idea bothered me. The reality of the situation being, I was nothing but trouble, and Jackson would be much better off with anyone but me. Besides, he probably already had a girlfriend before I came along, except he'd said that he didn't. He didn't seem the type to lie about that.

I glanced at the window. The sun was out today and spring was just around the corner. I took a deep breath and knew it was time. It seemed like a great day to venture out and get some stuff at the store.

I still wasn't quite sure about showing my face around this small town, but I'd gone through most of the items Jackson had brought up for me. There were still some things left, but a girl can only take so much pasta before she explodes from an overdose of carbs. Some fruits and vegetables were definitely on my shopping list, and I just didn't want to ask Jackson or Brodie to go to the store for me. I'd asked Jackson not to bring me anything else. I didn't want to keep using him that way, especially knowing that I'd made the decision to leave at the end of the month. It was hard to get him to agree, but once I told him I needed to start fending for myself and taking care of myself if I ever wanted to succeed in this new life he seemed so hell bent on me having, he backed down. Well, I didn't really say it that way, but I wanted to just so I could get it through his gorgeous skull that I didn't need any more of his help. He'd been coming on a little too strong. Not to the point that I didn't like it, I did like it, too much, and that was the problem. It appeared that he'd backed so far away now though I'd never see him. In fact, being up here by myself made me realize just how much I really did miss his company. Another reason I needed to leave.

I stood in the bathroom hardly recognizing the girl in the mirror. I still wasn't used to the blonde hair. I missed my long, dark auburn shade, and I didn't care much for the dark roots that were already visible only after a little over two weeks. I didn't know how I'd make it a whole month without a touch up. I might need to go see Leslie sooner than that, but I knew that would cost money, and I didn't start working at the bar until next Monday. I wanted to wait until all the bruising on my face went completely away before I started working. No matter how much Jackson said he liked the color of my hair, I still thought it made me look a little washed out and fake. I had to admit it did make me look completely different though, and might just help keep Troy from finding me.

I got dressed, and put on a bit of make-up; managing to cover almost all of the bruising that was mostly a yellowish color now, but still visible. Maybe I could start working at the bar sooner. Jackson mentioned that he wanted me to start on a slow night though, and since today was Friday, I'd most likely still need to wait until Monday. I pulled my hair back into a ponytail, which showed the dark roots at the hairline of my forehead, so I quickly took that out. God, I hated this. Maybe bangs? Nah. I hated those too. Then I'd always need to have them cut. I was a simple girl and hated the idea of "needing" to go have my hair done all the time. Only, I knew the blonde hair was a necessary evil, one that just might save my life.

I grabbed my keys and went out onto the landing. I turned to lock the door, making sure it was secure by pulling on it, and then headed down to my car. Jackson stood at the bottom of the stairs, one foot on the first step as if he'd been on his way up. My heart danced a little and my stomach did a little flippity flop at the sight of his gorgeous face.

Chapter 31
Jackson

Wow, I didn't realize how much I'd actually missed watching Lena's pretty face heal. She just got more beautiful every day.

We both kind of just stood there staring at each other for a few minutes until she finally said, "Jackson." My name sounded like sweet music flowing from her lips.

"Hi."

"Hi," she said, walking down toward me.

"Where are you going?" Okay, even I thought that sounded a little too nosy, but I couldn't help myself. She was so fragile still.

"Um …"

"Sorry, I didn't mean to pry." I took my foot off the step, feeling like a fool. I'd wanted to see her so badly, and I couldn't stand to stay away for one more second. I'd never dreamed that she'd be taking off to go somewhere.

"No, no, you're not prying at all. I'm going to the store for some fruit. There are only so many potatoes and pasta dishes a girl can handle. After a while, she starts to bloat." She laughed at her little joke, but now I felt horrible about leaving her up there with nothing but carbohydrates for three days.

"Sorry, I uh … I should have been more considerate." What the hell was wrong with me? I was acting like I hadn't spoken to a woman in a year.

She smiled. "No worries. I'm just going to drive over to the grocery store."

She walked passed me, and her scent had me entranced as I blurted out, "Want me to drive you?"

She paused, looking at me over her shoulder. "No. That's okay. I think it's time I start figuring out how to get around in this town on my own."

"You're probably right."

"Thanks, though." She got in her car and started the engine but didn't go anywhere. She rolled down her window. "Jack?"

"Yeah." I hurried over to her car.

"How do I get to the store?"

We both broke out in laughter at that.

"Why don't I just hop in and go with you this

time?"

She sighed, and I could tell she really wanted to try to do it on her own, but realized she couldn't yet. "Well, okay. This time."

I practically ran, sliding into the passenger side and buckled up. I glanced over at her smiling face. "I'm sure there will be plenty of other times in the future for you to proclaim your independence." I don't know why I said that. The smile on her face changed to a frown, and I instantly regretted the comment.

She put the car in reverse and began backing out. "It's easier if you just go forward and go around that tree and head out."

"Oh. You're right. I didn't realize that was a possibility." She giggled, but it sounded more like nervous energy. I gave her the rest of the directions as we went. The traffic began to build up the closer we got to town, which was a bit unusual for this small community.

"Wow, is there always this much traffic down here?"

"No. Never. I wonder what's ... unless ... oh, yeah."

"What?"

"I forgot. It's Founder's Day. Good thing I came along. Wow this is crazy. I've never seen it this crowded before. Take a left down this alley. We'll take a shortcut." She turned, but the police had the alley barricaded off at the end, and cars blocked our way behind us. We were stuck. "Sorry, it doesn't look as if we can get out for a while."

She pulled over to the side of the alley. "So, what now?"

"Well … when's the last time you went to a parade?"

She smiled. "Not since I was a kid."

"Well, sweetheart, what are you waiting for? Let's go."

Chapter 32

Lena

I was a little hesitant about getting out of the car. Going to the grocery store was one thing, but being out on the street with so many people frightened me a bit. Jackson walked beside me, his hand at the small of my back, coaxing me down the alley toward the music of the marching band. I did not, for a second, relax the entire time his fingers guided me along. The pressure of his touch on my back was exhilarating, a somewhat new emotion, or at least one I hadn't experienced in a very long time.

We made our way up the sidewalk, weaving our way through the wall-to-wall people facing the street. The crowd was exciting to see. We found a spot by the curb to stand and watch as the band blasted out Carly Rae Jespen's "Call Me Maybe", and the cheers and shouts of all the onlookers rang through the very core of my body. People danced on the sidewalk and in the street behind the band. When the bandleader threw her baton up in the air and caught it without missing a beat, everyone cheered even louder. Behind the band came a fire truck decorated with American flags. Several attractive firefighters hung on the outside waving their hands, and a Dalmatian barked with excitement. It looked like a scene taken right out of a Norman Rockwell picture. Jackson yelled out to someone in the parade, "Hey, Donkey!" and laughed and splayed his hands out in front of him, palms up in a 'what the hell?' type of gesture. Jackson shook his head. I looked up to see Brodie standing across the street just outside of Jackson's bar. I assumed the donkey reference sparked from the conversation they'd had about me the other day when Jackson told Brodie he was an ass.

A little while later, Jackson yelled out, "Yo, Grail!" and gave the guy on the float a thumbs up. "Lookin' good, Grail!" he added before leaning his head close to mine. "That is our illustrious new mayor, and a good friend of mine, Tom Grail. He's only twenty-eight, and used to come into the bar a lot when my uncle owned it. He still comes in, but not as much now. "Mayoral duties.'" Jackson raised both hands and wiggled his two fingers in the air as he said the words, mayoral duties. "The 'Holy Grail,' that's what a lot of people call him now days. He has done a lot for this small town. Good things too." Jackson got this little gleam in his eye when he spoke about his friend. He never seemed to hide any emotions from me. I liked that. It revealed so much about him, and I admired his candidness.

More shouts and cheers rang out around us as a small float, looking something like a huge turtle, came into view. The town's mascot I presumed. The turtle's head bobbed up and down, swaying from side to side. "Oh, my, God!" I said as streams of confetti spewed from the turtle's mouth and fell from the sky around us. Little strands of paper and dots of red, purple, orange and green attached themselves to our hair and clothes. Jackson scooped me up in his arms, twirling me around and around. I giggled uncontrollably, and when he put me back on the ground, he kissed me.

And time stopped for a few seconds.

I think for both of us.

The kiss ended almost as quickly as it started. He pulled away, dropping his arms to his sides, realizing what he'd done. The music, the shouts and cheers around us became a sound in the distance as we simply stared at each other. It hadn't been a long kiss, more just a peck really, but a kiss nonetheless.

The rest of the parade seemed to happen in a fog for me as all I could think about after that was Jackson's kiss and what it had meant. Small as it was, and most likely insignificant to him, I didn't quite know how to interpret it. I'm sure it was just a fun little kiss to show his excitement about the parade, but then why did he suddenly push me away and stare at me? Maybe I'd been giving it too much importance, but it stirred something in me. Something I wanted to experience again, and maybe a little longer next time. That thought scared me. I couldn't let myself fall for Jackson. I had to keep running.

After about another thirty minutes, the parade came to an end. "We should get going." Jackson turned to go, and I followed. "It's going to get a little crazy around here," he shouted over his shoulder, then took my hand in his. "Stay close."

We weaved in and out of people. I almost had to run to keep up with Jackson's long stride. He didn't stop or slow down even when we came to a group of teenagers taking up the entire sidewalk. He simply headed for the street and hurried around them. I almost tripped on the curb, and thought I heard someone call my name. I tensed and turned to look behind me. Who would be calling me here in this town? "Lena!" I heard again, but couldn't see anyone I knew. I started to panic, but then thought maybe it was Leslie, but she knew me as Lana, not Lena. Besides Jackson, she was the only one that knew me here, other that Brodie and Doc, and it was a female voice. "Lena!" There it was again, and I turned to see a woman grabbing a little girl about eight years old by the hand. "Lia! Please don't walk so far ahead in this crowd. I don't want to lose you."

I released a huge breath of relief and fought to keep up with Jackson. She'd been shouting for Lia, not Lena.

My jittery soul could relax, but not too much, I reminded myself. Troy had a magical talent for finding people who wanted to stay hidden.

Chapter 33

Jackson

As I pulled Lena along, I kept thinking about the kiss. It had been a stupid thing to do, but she just looked so inviting with that gorgeous smile and all that confetti floating around us, I guess I got caught up in the excitement. I had nothing to say afterwards, which was also stupid. I could have at least said I was sorry, but then that would have been a lie. At least I'd managed not to make it too much like a romantic kiss, which is what I'd really wanted to do. For the brief moment that my lips touched hers, I did get a sense of how soft they were, and the whole small yet so large moment, overwhelmed me. I wanted more.

But that wasn't going to happen. Not any time

soon, I guessed, from the way she reacted; which was more like she didn't react, a total and complete blow to my ego. I held on tightly to her hand as we made our way through the crowd, wondering what she'd been thinking. She kept looking behind her. "What's wrong?" I asked.

"Nothing. I thought … nothing. It's nothing," she said, shaking her head.

As we got closer to the alley where we'd left the car, the crowd cleared, and we slowed down to an easy pace. I realized I should let go of her hand. I didn't want to, but I did.

Neither one of us said anything when we got back into the car. I worried that I really blew it. I should have known she wasn't ready. After a couple of minutes of excruciating silence, Lena said," That was fun."

I looked over, and she was smiling. "Yeah, it was. I'd forgotten that today was Founder's Day. This town usually has some sort of recognition, but the parade is something new, and I'm sure that the "Holy Grail" had something to do with it. Oh, here's the store."

We pulled into the parking lot of Staples. Not the Staples with all the office supplies, but the little family owned grocery store named after old man Staples, one of the town's founding fathers. It was the only grocery store in Turtle Lake. "There is a brand new Railey's that popped up last year in Fall River Valley, which is only a couple of miles away. They'd tried to build here in Turtle Lake," I explained, "but the town's residents fought hard to keep it out, so they settled for the next town over. I like to shop here though; we need to support our local businesses if we want to keep our small town alive."

I pushed the cart and followed Lena down the aisles as she grabbed some apples and broccoli and mushrooms. She picked up a basket of strawberries and glanced at the price sign, then put them back on the shelf. She did this with a few other items and after about ten minutes; I realized there weren't many groceries in the cart. I figured she didn't have much money, and I so wanted to pay for these groceries, but somehow I didn't think she'd let me.

We left the produce department and headed toward the meats. She stood over the chicken, studying it, picking up several different containers, placing them back before settling on one.

"Hmmm … what's for dinner?" I asked.

"Chicken Marsala, I think."

"You know how to make that?"

She nodded. "Do you like it?"

"Yeah. I guess. I've never had it."

"Well, I make a pretty tasty Marsala. I'm sure I can make enough for you and Brodie to have some tonight."

"Wow. That would be awesome."

We headed to the wines, and she picked up a bottle of Marsala. She held it in her hand, biting on her bottom lip and stuck it in the cart. Good thing it only cost three ninety-nine or she probably would have put it back. But then, I would have offered to pay for it if she had.

We headed home and the drive was much less stressful without the parade going on. "Do you mind if we stop at the bar before going home?"

"Not at all."

"I want to pick up a bottle of wine to go with that chicken. What time's dinner, I'll let Brodie know?"

"Um … I'll bring it down around seven. Is that okay?"

"Oh, sorry. I thought you'd make it downstairs, and we could all have dinner together."

"Oh." She frowned and chewed her lip again, and I knew I was pushing it, but then I wanted to jump and shout hooray, when she said, "Okay," but I refrained.

"Good. I'll be right back." I left her there in the car with the motor running in case I needed a good excuse to leave right away. I grabbed a bottle of Zin, and then grabbed another. We didn't have any wine at home, and if Brodie was joining us, I figured we'd need it.

"What's with the wine?" Brodie said as I placed the two bottles in a bag I found under the counter.

"Lena is going to cook tonight. You're invited," I said.

"I have a date, but thanks."

"Whose got the bar?"

"Derrick."

"Okay. Where are you going?" I wasn't really all that curious about Brodie's date, but since he wasn't going to join us for dinner, I wanted to know how much alone time I'd have with Lena tonight.

"Really? You really want to know? You're only asking so you'll know what time I'll be home." He shook his head, and I knew he had me pegged. There was no way he was going to tell me.

I headed out to the car, keeping both bottles of wine anyway. I wasn't sure if I should mention to Lena that Brodie wasn't joining us, but then I didn't want to deceive her that way. "Brodie has a date and won't be joining us for dinner," I blurted out unable to hide the silly grin on my face.

Chapter 34

Lena

I really wasn't surprised when Jackson said that Brodie wouldn't be joining us for dinner. He had a date almost every night when he wasn't working the bar. "Smells good," he'd said when he strolled into the kitchen right before leaving. He stuck his finger in the sauce and put it to his lips. "It is good. Now I'm almost sorry I have other plans."

I didn't say anything. I didn't know what to say. I'd felt uneasy around Brodie since walking into that conversation he'd had with Jackson before I moved upstairs.

"Lena," he paused, waiting for me to look at him.

"I'm sorry about the things I said last week."

"It's okay."

"No, it's not. I'm not a mean guy … normally.

"Normally?"

"I mean, I just worry about my brother."

"Well you needn't worry. There's nothing going on between us."

He frowned. "That's debatable, but not the point. I like you, and just want you to know that what I said the other day, well, it was nothing personal."

"It felt personal." God, where'd Jackson go? I did not want to have this conversation with Brodie right now. Or anytime. Ever.

"I'm sorry. I guess what I'm trying to say is, Jackson tends to … well, obsess about helping people. I just don't want him to get hurt you know."

We all knew the possibilities of Troy finding me and causing a world of trouble for not only me, but them, as well.

"Well, don't worry. I won't let that happen. I haven't told Jackson yet, but I'll be leaving at the end of next month after I've made enough money to pay you both back for your hospitality, and also make enough to get me back on the road."

He took a step back, his eyes wide with surprise. "Oh."

"Let's keep that to ourselves though if you don't mind. Otherwise, you and I both know that Jack will spend the entire month trying to coax me to stay."

"Right. I guess you know him better than I thought

you did, but you also know that's going to hurt him."

"I'll try my best to keep things casual. I like him, but not that way," I lied. "And I don't want to hurt him."

The chicken Marsala turned out perfect. Not tasting too much like wine, with just enough butter to give it a creamy texture. I'd learned to make it perfect for Troy or he'd have rewarded me with a backhand across my cheek.

We ate in silence. The wine Jackson brought home went very well with it too. He must have liked it because I caught him scraping his fork over every last drop of sauce on his plate.

"The parade was fantastic today. I'm so glad we didn't miss it," I said, breaking the silence.

"That would have been a shame. I'm glad we caught it, too. Wow, Lena, that was fantastic. I am now, officially, a chicken Marsala fan."

I stood to clear the dishes from the table and Jackson joined in to help. I didn't quite know how to react to that at first since it was something Troy would have never dreamed of doing. I don't know why I was so surprised about Jack's willingness to help tonight. He'd done everything every other night, and it had been me offering to help him, which at first he wouldn't let me do because of my injuries. I was healed now. The side of my back still hurt a bit where Troy kicked me, but nothing like it first did.

There were only a few things left to clean up, and I was looking forward to going back upstairs and collapsing into bed. It had been my first day out, and I was exhausted.

"After we finish cleaning up, I need to do some practicing. You can join me if you'd like. I'll go build a fire, dancing flames seem to help me think," Jackson said.

"Oh." I was tired, but the prospect of listening to him play, and me jamming along, was too much to pass up. "Okay. Go ahead out and I'll finish up here."

After wiping down the counter until it was spotless, another rule of Troy's, I went into the living room to find Jackson in the big easy chair, guitar in hand, the fire roaring. My fingers practically itched with the anticipation of strumming the chords on his spare guitar. And there it was, leaning against the side of the sofa. Jackson looked up and smiled. "Go on. Pick it up."

A force much greater than I had the power to fight—not that I would have—made me walk over to the sofa and pick up that guitar. I sat with it, and within a few minutes, we were deep into that song Jackson taught me the other night. He'd said he'd written it, but he'd yet to sing the lyrics aloud, and I knew he had some because I'd seen him with this notebook jotting down words as he'd played it. I wondered what it was about.

"When are you going to let me hear the words to

this?" I asked, hoping I wasn't being too forward or prying. After all, I knew from experience that song lyrics could be very personal sometimes, and the way he always hid them from Brodie and me, I figured these must be pretty private.

"Oh. They aren't quite ready, yet."

"I can't wait to hear them because I love the tune." His lips curved up on one side, and I got the impression that he was proud of the ones he'd written so far. I didn't press him about it any further. We played for about an hour, shooting ideas back and forth, and he really seemed to like everything I suggested. I'd been nursing the same glass of wine I'd had at dinner, and finally took the last sip. I didn't drink much; I never wanted to after witnessing Troy make a big fool of himself so many times, or how nasty he became whenever we were alone. But right now, in this moment, I wanted another glass of wine, mainly because I didn't want the night to end. I was having such a great time. I stood. "I'll get some more wine, would you like another glass?"

"Sure."

I headed to the kitchen, and realized he'd followed me in there. I reached out for the bottle, and his hand came over mine. "Allow me." He smiled, and I pulled my hand away. He stood close and poured the wine. He held my glass up for me to take, but when I reached for it, he took my hand into his free one and placed the glass back on the counter. He stood facing me, and our gazes locked.

"The lyrics are about you, Lena," he confessed, and I watched his mouth as the tip of his tongue moistened his lips before he leaned his head down. Then those beautiful lips were on mine, soft, tender at first, then his tongue glided over my lips, breaking the seal. My pulse throbbed and quickened as his tongue swirled around mine. Taking and controlling, and … and I wanted this, needed his touch. I went limp in his embrace, and the heat rose under my skin, my body vibrated against his strong powerful one. Was this really happening? I reached up and ran my fingers through his thick hair while his hand slipped under my shirt, his fingers grazing my side below my rib cage. I forced Troy's wicked face from my mind, but it was no use. Would I always have his hateful glare in my thoughts every time I tried to be with another man? Maybe it was better for Jackson's sake that I did. Brodie's words rang loud and clear in my head, and I once again shoved my hand against Jackson's chest putting several inches between us.

Chapter 35
Jackson

*L*ena slowly shook her head, a tear escaping from one of her eyes, and I stepped toward her, brushing it away with my thumb. My fingers held her cheek as her gaze fell to the floor. "Jackson, I …"

I pulled her close against me and tilted her chin up, giving me access to her lips. "I'm sorry, Lena," I said. "I'm so very sorry he hurt you. I'm not him. I won't hurt you I promise. I will never hurt you."

Her lips parted as I said all those words, our mouths mere centimeters apart, and she sighed into me, surrendering to me as if those words held some magic potion in them. I held her close until there was no space between us, as though I couldn't get close enough. She opened her mouth and allowed me in. The tip of my tongue brushed softly against hers, and I let her reach out for mine. I didn't want to hurt her or take what she didn't want to give. I wanted to be careful with her, more careful than I'd ever been with a woman in my entire life. I'd never cared or thought about what I took before. A kiss had always been just a kiss, never meaning much. This time, I cared because Lena deserved it. She deserved to be kissed the way a woman should be kissed, with tenderness and respect, but I couldn't keep the heat out.

We continued the kiss. I didn't want to stop, ever, but I knew if we didn't we'd soon be doing more than just kissing. Well, at least that's what I would have wanted. Lena, on the other hand, wasn't ready. I knew this. After what seemed like too little time as far as I was concerned, she slowly pulled away.

We just stood there in the kitchen. I waited for her to say something, but instead of talking about what just happened, she walked out of the kitchen, grabbed her keys, and left, slowly shutting the door. I listened to the quickness of her steps as she ran up the stairs to the cottage.

I didn't know what to do. She'd been through so much with that monster jerk she'd married. She'd been wronged beyond comprehension in the worse possible way, and she needed time, healing time before I thought she'd be ready for me. She needed time, space. I knew that, and I'd give it to her, but damn it, it was painful to do.

Chapter 36
Lena

I stood with my back against the door and sank down to the floor. My God, what just happened? I couldn't believe I let Jackson kiss me. Just earlier in the evening I'd made a promise to Brodie, and myself, that I wouldn't get involved with Jackson that way.

I skimmed my finger over my lips, remembering his touch, the texture, the taste. Jackson's lips had been so soft; he'd been so tender and loving. I could tell he was holding back the second time because of the way he let me take control. The first kiss had been more urgent, but the second, the second kiss was tender and caring. I'd never been kissed like that before. I licked my lips and thought about what to do.

Oh God, I wanted him so much.

I got up, yanked off my clothes and got into the sweat pants and T-shirt that belonged to Jackson so I could have him close to me. I reached over and flipped on the iPod he'd lent me and climbed under the covers, bringing them up under my chin; a poor substitute for Jackson's warm body. Music always soothed my spirit, and it was comforting to sleep by, particularly the Christina Perri album he'd downloaded to it. As the song, "Arms" played softly, I wrapped my own around my shoulders and thought about Jackson's strong biceps, pretending he was right there beside me, rocking me to sleep.

But I couldn't sleep. How could I sleep thinking about that kiss and the song he said was about me. I couldn't believe he thought about me that much to write a song. I laid there for about fifteen minutes more, and decided to get up and make some tea.

Chapter 37
Jackson

Five minutes after Lena ran upstairs, Brodie came home. I was glad he missed the show.

"Hey," I said, and he grunted as he walked to the fridge. Something was off. "What's going on?"

He turned toward me, holding a bag of peas to his face.

"What the hell happened to you?" I asked.

"Some joker thought he'd use my face for a punching bag, that's what happened. Parades seem to bring the worst, as well as the best, out of people, and some of them can't hold their liquor, particularly when their wife is cheating on them."

"You were with a married woman?"

"She was here for the parade from Fall River Valley, and I didn't know she was married. She lied about that."

"Ya think?"

He gave me a sour look. "Don't judge."

I laughed. "I won't judge you if you don't judge me, little brother."

He gave me a side-ways glare. "What happened now?"

"I kissed Lena tonight," I blurted it out, too excited about it not to.

"She's still married."

"Legally separated as of three days ago, and what about not judging?"

"Okay. Well, it was bound to happen, I guess."

"That's all you're going to say?"

"You said not to judge."

"I know, but I still want your opinion."

"No, you don't. You only want it if it's something you want to hear."

He had a point, so I let it go. I knew how he felt about it, and I didn't want to hear it, but I'd hoped that because of his messed up evening, he'd try to see things a little differently. Brodie had a bizarre way of dealing with things. I knew this by the way he used women. In his mind, he wasn't doing anything wrong, just having fun. But I knew what tormented my little brother.

I couldn't stand not knowing how Lena was feeling

about the kiss, and I couldn't stand not knowing whether or not she hated me now. So I drove into town and picked up some sticky buns from Traci's Bakery. Luckily, I caught Traci just as she was locking up for the night.

I knocked on Lena's door, and she opened it a crack.

"Hi," I held up the pink box. "We never had dessert." I gave her the most charming smile I had. "And these are the best cinnamon buns in the entire county, something everyone should try at least once. And it's my way of saying 'thank you' for dinner." That was all true, but it was also my excuse to see her.

I'm sure she saw through my lame excuse after I'd said it by the way she smiled and slowly opened the door wider for me to enter. She turned toward the kitchen. "I just finished boiling some water for tea. I'll get us a cup."

I set the box of pastries on the small coffee table and watched her in the kitchen. She'd changed into the sweatpants I'd given her. I wondered if she slept in them, and had to pull myself from the vision of her under the sheets, without the pants. We sat at the table, drank the tea and ate the sticky buns, avoiding any and all discussion about the kiss, but I knew we were both thinking about it.

After a short while, "Distance" by Christina Perri and Jason Marz played softly in the background from the iPod station I'd lent her. The songs on it were my collection, and I knew them well. Such an appropriate song for our situation. It was almost as if the iPod knew I was coming up, and wanted to give me a message. The unspoken tension between us was deafening, and when the song changed to another on the same album, I couldn't help myself as Christina Perri's voice gave me all the instructions I needed and I put my arms around Lena and held her close as we swayed to the words of "Arms."

When the song ended, I led her over to the small bed/sofa. Without saying anything, she sat down, and I sat next to her. She rested her head on my shoulder and I draped my arm around her.

"Will you tell me the words?"

"The words?"

"The lyrics. To the song you're writing."

"Ah ..." Was I ready to reveal them? I shuffled my body so that she'd be more comfortable. "My guitar is all the way downstairs."

She sighed heavily. "Can't you just say the words?"

"I guess," I said, and picked up her hand, rubbing my thumb over her fingers as I spoke.

Fleeing demons from the past
Only to find she can't escape
Her wounds are deep, scars are masked
By her pain as she moves too late

Fleeing demons from the past

Beautifully Wounded

She longs for days without the pain
Healing wings for hope at last
When ev'ry turn, it seems the same

All her fears can fall away
Now that she's right here with me

I felt the wetness of her tears on my shirt.

"Come on, baby, you're exhausted." I helped her stretch out onto the bed. I knew she had to be tired after the busy day; it being her first day out. I pulled the cover over her and slid in next to her, holding on to her. At first, I thought she might object, but when she scooted her body up against mine, fitting hers into every curve of mine as if we were molded together, I realized that I shouldn't have worried. She didn't need to comment on the lyrics, I wasn't looking for anything, I only hoped she understood them. When she began to sob, my heart broke, and I knew she had. She cried for a while, and I held her close. We stayed like that for the rest of the night, her sleeping in my arms.

Chapter 38
Lena

It was finally Monday. I thought it would never come. Jackson spent the next two nights with me upstairs, and he put the music to the beautiful lyrics he'd written. It was amazing how he got me. The comfort of his body next to mine while I slept was amazing. I managed to leave the hammer on the floor instead of under my pillow, now. I didn't think I'd be able to sleep without him again. He never tried to kiss me again, but I knew he wanted to. He was the kindest, most understanding man I'd ever met. Well, I didn't know many, but my track record up until then hadn't exactly been the best, other than Weezer. But Weezer was just a friend. Not someone I'd ever want to be sleeping next to me. He'd been too much like an older brother, always trying to protect me, and sometimes, I had to admit, worrying about me. I suppose I should have listened to him when he begged me not to marry Troy. He'd been right, but never, ever said those awful I-told-you-so words. I realized that Weezer and Jackson were a lot alike. Except Weezer always treated me like a little sister, and with Jackson, there was never any I-want-to-be-your-brother attitude going on. With Jackson, I always got I-think-you're-hot-and-want-to-hold-you-next-to-me kind of vibes.

My first day at the bar went by without a hitch. Brodie had me clearing tables and delivering drinks mostly. He actually seemed pleased to have me there, and was more than willing to go out of his way to make me feel comfortable. I'd wondered what I'd done to change his mind about me. There weren't very many customers, so the day sort of dragged on, but I was happy to be out and seeing what little of the community I did. Jackson said that Mondays were busier during the football season, but assured me that once the hockey playoffs started in April, business would pick up again.

The days were flying by, and most nights after work, Jackson let me use his spare guitar, and we played together. We usually played down at his place, but I always insisted that I go upstairs to sleep, and even though Jackson insisted on coming with me, claiming that he knew I slept better when he was there—I couldn't argue with that—I still wanted to go upstairs to give Brodie the privacy I knew he wanted.

Brodie liked having a variety of women at his disposal, bringing many of them home to spend the night, and made no apologies for his actions. In spite of his sexual habits, I actually started to like Brodie, and I think the feeling was mutual. I worried about his promiscuity, but I'd never had the nerve to mention it. That was Jackson's job, but he only got on his case jokingly, though I knew from conversations we'd had that he didn't think Brodie was doing himself any favors with the way he treated the ladies. He wasn't mean to them at all, in fact, from what I'd witnessed, Brodie was extremely sweet to them, just noncommittal. Brodie was handsome, looking similar to Jackson, so I understood the lure, but I didn't understand the *why*. Local girls knew about Brodie's lechery and still flocked to his side, wanting his attention. They still came home with him, knowing that he'd most likely be with someone else the very next night. Jackson had joked more than once that Brodie should take out stock in one of the larger, well-known condom companies.

The month flew by, and before I knew it, I was waiting tables and taking orders as if I'd been doing it my entire life. I was having a blast. Before I knew it, one month turned into two, and I hadn't forgotten about my promise to myself to leave after I'd paid Jackson and Brodie back for their hospitality. I was just sad that I needed to leave. It was going to be one of the hardest things for me to do. Jackson and I spent every night together playing songs, and then later retreating upstairs to sleep, but usually the first thirty minutes or so of that turned into a grand make out session. We'd never go any further than kissing. He'd never pushed me to go any further, and quite frankly, I didn't think I was ready anyway.

Friday nights were the busiest at the bar, and Jackson usually played with his band. I walked slowly across the room, a tray balancing on the palm of my hand as Jackson began to speak through the mic and the entire room grew quiet.

"I have a treat for you all," he began, a smile twitched on his face. We have a lovely guest performance tonight." My eyes instantly flicked up to the stage to see whom he might be talking about, and he was looking right at me. My face grew hot even before he said my name. Well, he used my fake name, but still. "Ladies and Gents, if you will, help me give a warm welcome to the lovely, Lana Martin." My heart leaped into my throat and I shook my head. "Come on up here, baby, let's show these folks what an angel sounds like."

I just stood, staring at him until someone took the tray from me. I smiled briefly in surprise and looked back up at the stage. People started yelling and clapping, and then I felt a hand at my back giving me a little push. I turned around to see Brodie smiling at me. "Go ahead," he coaxed as he stood there holding the tray I'd been carrying.

I walked slowly up the steps, taking Jackson's

outstretched hand. I sat on the chair next to him and strapped on the guitar he handed me. "You ready?" he asked. I nodded.

We sang one of the songs we'd been practicing, the Christine Perri and Jason Marz duet of *Distance*. It had become one of our favorites to sing together, and one he knew I was very familiar with. After the song, everyone in the bar stood and clapped. "See that, baby? That's for you. A standing ovation."

I beamed, proudly. I'd missed performing so much, and that night made me remember why.

Chapter 39

Jackson

I couldn't have been more proud of Lena. She stayed up on stage with us and performed two more numbers. I'd brought home a bottle of champagne to celebrate, and as we entered the cottage, I flipped on the light and stared at the small bed. I'd been sleeping up here holding on to Lena every night, but I had to admit, I missed my own bed. I wanted to stay with her, but I didn't relish sleeping in that tiny bed tonight.

"Lena."

She turned to me and wrapped her arms around my neck. "Yes?" she said with a grin that seemed permanently put on her face ever since that first song we performed, and I was damn glad to see it. I didn't want to ruin anything, but I needed a good night's sleep. "Will you come with me downstairs to my place? Sleep there tonight?"

She followed my eyes to the small sofa we'd been sharing. "What, you don't like snuggling close on that?"

"I love snuggling close, but I'd also love to do it in a bigger bed where my ass isn't hanging off the edge.

She giggled then let out a heavy sigh. "I love sleeping with you Jackson. And I love what we do before we go to sleep, but if I go downstairs it would be like me living down there again, and Brod ..."

"Don't worry about Brodie," I interrupted. "He's changed his mind about you now that he's seen the light ..."

"And what light would that be?"

He leaned his forehead against mine. "The light that glows from the top of your head like an angel's halo when you sing."

I laughed. "Now I have a halo? You must have been standing behind me when I was looking in the mirror or something because I think the shine came from your own halo."

"Well, now that we've established that we are both celestial beings, can we please go stroke each other's feathers in my bed?"

"Okay. Just let me get my stuff."

I let out a puff of air, and helped her to gather her sweatpants and stuff.

The house was dark, which meant Brodie was still

at the bar. Good. Even though I'd said he changed his tune about Lena, I still didn't want to run into him on our way to my room. It was only eleven, and I knew Brodie would be out until at least one in the morning. The bar closed at two o'clock, but Brodie liked to let Derrick close on Friday nights so he could have some fun with a girl, and from what I knew, Friday nights were his best chance for that.

"Lena, before we go to sleep, I have another surprise, and another reason to drink this champagne tonight."

"What is it?"

"Luke managed to get the judge to expedite the divorce and emailed the final papers to me this morning."

"Really?" she gaped at me. "But I thought it would take ninety days? It's only been forty." She said that like she knew the exact date and time everything would be final, and quite frankly, I bet she did.

"Usually, there is a ninety-day waiting period between the time he'd been served and the final judgment, but because of the circumstances, the fact that you'd been married under a year and the abuse, Luke was able to convince the judge to waive the ninety-day period and expedite the final papers. Here they are." I handed her the copy I printed. "The originals should be here any day now, but Luke emailed these to me this morning."

"Oh my God. I'm really free?"

God, the way she said "free" broke my heart. As though she'd been held prisoner by the jerk. Well, I guess she had been. "Yeah, sweetheart, you're free."

Tears streamed down her cheeks, and she sobbed. "Why are you crying? I thought you would be happy."

"I am, I am so happy. So grateful to you."

"You are now, officially, a single woman." I smiled, pulled her close to me and held her. No one could have been happier than I was that she was no longer married to that creep.

After she'd shed all the "happy" tears she had, I popped the cork on the bottle of bubbly and we toasted to her newfound independence.

"Let's take this into the bedroom. I'd really like to get comfortable and cozy," I suggested, and she nodded, clinking her glass against mine another time.

I set the bottle of champagne and the two glasses on the nightstand, and she took her clothes and went into the bathroom to change. I had yet to see her fully naked. I'd had my hands on almost every part of her body, but never directly on her soft skin. I knew it was soft, because, although I hadn't actually fondled her naked body completely, my hands and lips were no stranger to her stomach, shoulders, and neck. I'd never tried to go any further than that, not while she was still married. I pulled my shirt off just as she walked out of the bathroom. Though it hadn't been the first time she'd ever seen me without a shirt, her eyes grew a bit wider as she stared at me this time. She stared so hard even the tattoos on my arms and chest began to feel self-conscious. Maybe, because this was the first time she'd seen me standing without my pants too. The other shirtless times I'd at least had jeans on. I glanced down at the blue and white striped boxers I had on, wondering if she thought they looked stupid or sexy. "Um ..." she averted her eyes and walked to the dresser to set her clothes on top of it. Her back was to me now.

I slid under the sheets without saying a word, and she turned around and smiled. She wore the heavy sweatpants and the same T-shirt I'd given her when she first moved in upstairs. The same ones she wore every night. "I'm gonna need to get you some new pjs, woman. Aren't you tired of wearing those?"

She laughed. "No. I like wearing your clothes."

"Yeah, but you've been wearing the same ones for two months now."

"Well, I do wash them every few days."

"But it's getting warmer now, and we have this heavy comforter on here. You're going to roast in those." I got out of bed and walked to the dresser, pulled out a new T-shirt, one that had a picture of a guitar on it and printed underneath, the words, "guitarists finger faster." Realizing what it said, I shoved it back in the drawer and pulled out another plain white one, along with a pair of purple, yes purple, silk boxers.

"Purple?"

"What, you don't like purple?"

"Yeah, I like purple." She smiled. "What was

wrong with the other shirt with the picture of the guitar?" She reached into the drawer for the other shirt and held it up to read. Her cheeks flushed pink and she wadded the shirt up into a ball, shoving it back in the drawer. "The plain white one will do fine, thanks."

I closed the drawer and took her hand, leading her away before she discovered some other things in my dresser that might make her change her mind about sleeping with me in my bed. I never claimed to be a virgin, or a saint.

"Go change."

I got back in bed and waited. She came out looking a little fresher and cooler, turned off the light next to the bed and got in beside me. I'd left the small night light on in the outlet on the wall and it glowed, giving the room a nice warm golden ambiance; just enough light for drinking champagne by, or for kissing.

We sat up with our backs propped up against the headboard and sipped some more of the bubbly stuff. It was good, cool and refreshing. Lena giggled a little and wiped her finger under her nose. "The bubbles got me," she admitted.

I took the glass from her and placed it on the table beside me along with mine, then took her face in my hands. "You are so beautiful." She opened her mouth slightly as if she was about to object, or maybe she just didn't know what to say, but I didn't give her a chance as I covered her lips with mine. Taking full advantage of her open mouth, I slipped my tongue inside, tasting the wine and her, reveling in her willingness to allow me to kiss her. One of her hands slid up my back, and I moved my hand down to her waist and under the shirt. I skimmed my finger along her stomach, waiting for her to stop me. Instead of stopping me, she pressed her fingers against my chest and slowly rubbed them over my nipples, lingering there, teasing me. I thought I would explode. I'd been thinking about this woman being under me for so long, it had almost become, no not almost, it *had* become a fantasy; one I'd thought about every night. It was difficult for me to control my excitement, kissing her while lying in *my* bed, wearing nothing but boxer shorts. I wanted her, and I didn't know if I could contain myself any longer. Sleeping with her upstairs in that small bed fully clothed was so much easier. I swore that I wouldn't be the one to make the move, but man, this was killing me.

Chapter 40
Lena

I was single. I was single. I wasn't married to Troy anymore. I kept repeating the words to myself while Jackson and I kissed, trying to accept the reality. I couldn't believe how good it felt, and then my fingers found his chest and the soft hairs there, the firmness of his pecs. My fingers glided over the tattoo of the little guitar he had above his left pectoral muscle that I'd never been close enough to touch before. I skimmed them over to the side, and traced the outline of the small fawn he had. I'd need to ask him about that one some time.

"Jackson?" I spoke his name against his mouth.

"Yeah, baby, what is it?"

"Will you take me to get a tattoo tomorrow?"

He blinked. "Sure. Did you have something special in mind?"

"No, but I know I want one. Maybe something like a butterfly to start with, something that is free and butterflies are free."

"I think there is a movie about that or something."

"Oh ...well, maybe a bird, definitely something with wings."

"You could get wings etched across your shoulder blades, and then you truly will be like an angel." He laughed, and so did I. I'd seen photos of girls who'd done that. That wasn't really my style though.

"I don't think I'm quite ready for something that drastic."

We started kissing again, and I forgot about being single, or married, or being free. I just let my mind go, and enjoyed the texture of his skin, and the tight ripples of the muscles in his stomach. I walked my fingers up to his nipples, and found them firm and suckable; his breath hitched against my mouth.

I stopped kissing him and pulled away only about an inch or two, not because I was scared, but because I wanted to look at his face. I needed to see his expression when I asked the next question.

"Jackson?"

"Yes, sweetheart," he whispered, gazing into my eyes searching for whatever it was I was about to ask.

"Will you make love to me?"

He didn't say anything at first, just brushed a few

loose strands of hair from my eyes and stared into them. "I …" he stuttered, "I would love to make love to you. It is all I've thought about for the past two months."

"Really?" That didn't surprise me, but I didn't want him to know I'd been thinking about him thinking about me that way.

"Yeah, but are you sure?"

"I'm very sure," I said, nodding, and he kissed me, his hands gently coaxing my body down the bed until I was completely flat. He lay beside me, kissing my neck, moving down to my stomach. He raised the T-shirt up, and his lips moved up my torso. He stopped suddenly and stared at me. "What's wrong?" I asked, wondering if I smelled bad or something.

"Can I take off the T-shirt?" he asked.

I nodded, unable to form the approval on my lips. I sat up a bit, and he pulled it over my head. My arms instantly went up to cover my breasts. He smiled, gently pulling them away and carefully laid me back down. His hands were warm on my skin, and the next thing I knew, the silk boxers were off too. He pressed tender kisses all over my stomach, inching his way down to the soft mound of curls, and within seconds, he pleasured me in a way that Troy had never bothered with. I moaned, delighting in the unexpected attention. After several minutes of what I thought had to be heaven, he kissed his way back up my stomach, lingering right below my belly button. As he kissed me there, he slipped his own shorts down and kicked them off somewhere into the sheets. I felt his hardness as his naked body covered mine. He kissed my shoulder, my neck, then kissed my lips, a tender, but heated kiss, filled with an urgency that I couldn't help return. I wanted to feel him inside me more than I'd ever wanted to feel another man before, but then he stopped kissing me. "Just a sec."

He slid off me and hopped out of bed. "Where are you going?"

"Just a minute." I stared at his perfect bottom, the muscles in his back and his slender hips as he opened the top drawer of his dresser and hurried back. Ripping open a condom, he put it on and slipped back in on top of me. I closed my eyes, briefly, but quickly opened them. I loved looking at Jackson. His green eyes sparkled with promise and trust. Yes, trust. He'd proven himself very trustworthy in the first thirty minutes of our first meeting that morning in his bar, and I'd grown to trust him more and more every day. His lips were warm, soft, gently pressing against me, his tongue skimmed against mine and retreated, only to find mine again. Something flitted and rolled inside my stomach, flowing up through my chest and I grabbed on to Jackson's back and pulled him closer to me so that we were now flesh to flesh. My heart pulsed heavy against his as desire swept over my senses, and he took me with a care and tenderness I didn't realize any man could do. It wasn't sex. It was love. I'd never realized the difference before. I'd thought I'd loved, but this, this was so much deeper and stronger than anything I had felt before. I'd always thought that the act of love-making had to be hard and quick in order for the man to experience that point of ecstasy. I'd never actually gotten to that level before. Troy had always finished before I'd had the chance. Or maybe it was just that I wasn't being turned on the way I seemed to be this time, with Jackson.

Chapter 41
Jackson

The surreal sensation of finally holding Lena in my arms this way, being this close, made my heart pound. This was her first time with me, a time she would remember forever, I hoped. I wanted to make it that special. I wanted to take away her bruises, not the ones on her skin that were already gone, but the ones inside. The ones she still occasionally had nightmares about. I wanted her to fall for me the way I was falling for her. My God, I didn't think I could have fallen any harder.

When I pressed into her completely, and the movement intensified, her face flushed with heat. My own body heat rose throughout my entire being, and I thought I would go crazy with desire. The more I fell, the more I wanted.

I awoke to the sun glaring in through the window. I'd forgotten to close the blinds last night in all my excitement, and I turned away from the glare to find Lena's beautiful face an inch from mine. I smiled. I couldn't help it. I reached out to hold her, and she snuggled into my arms.

"Mmmm …" She opened her eyes and smiled, even scooted closer against me.

"Hey."

"Hey."

"Ready for your tattoo?"

"I think so. Though I haven't really decided on what yet."

"That's always a plus before going to the tattoo artist."

"Yeah." She grinned, and traced her finger over the fawn on my chest. "Jackson. Why do you have a fawn tattooed on your chest?"

"Well, when I was a kid I rescued a fawn from being caught up in a bunch of barbed wire in the woods. Her leg was broken. I took her home and nursed her back to health, but my dad made me let her go. I cried about it, and never forgave my father for taking her back into the wild. I probably would have forgiven him had he stuck around longer, but I never got the chance. He left my mom shortly after that, and was then killed in an auto accident a few years later. It was a hard lesson to learn that there are some things that you just can't keep no matter how much you want them. You have to let them go. I got the tattoo to help me remember them both; the actual fawn, and the lesson."

She bit her bottom lip and snuggled into me. "I think I just thought of the perfect tattoo."

We ate a quick breakfast of toast with peanut butter and coffee, and headed downtown to my favorite tattoo parlor run by our drummer, Kipper. Lena was surprised to see him, but seemed pleased when she realized he would be the one to etch her very first tat. She described what she wanted, and he said that would be a piece of cake.

After the tattoo session, it was only a short walk to the car, but we needed to go through town to get to it since it was Saturday and parking on the street was difficult to find, particularly in this part of town. I held Lena's hand as we walked by the flower shop, and I tugged her to a stop. "Wait." I pulled her inside with me and picked up a dozen red roses. Women loved flowers, and I wanted to let Lena know how happy she'd made me. By the look on her face, I must have succeeded. I vowed right then that if she ever agreed to live her life with me, I'd buy her flowers once a week just so I could see the smile they caused.

We decided to walk around the town for a while just to pass the time and enjoy each other's company. I loved holding her hand while we walked. We stopped in the café on the corner for some lunch, and she begged me to help her remove the bandage. Kipper said it should stay on for one to three hours and it had been an hour and a half, so I removed it. The tattoo was gorgeous. Kipper really did a great job. A little later, we walked into the bar. Lena wanted to show off her new tattoo. She'd worn the perfect top that exposed her left shoulder, yet still had long sleeves to keep her warm. It was still early spring and the temperature fluctuated throughout the day, cooling down to forty degrees some nights. Lena walked up to the bar, turned her back toward Brodie and Derrick, and let her coat drape down her arm revealing her bared shoulder and the new four-inch tattoo of the winged guitar.

Even though the sun was still shining, you could never tell inside the bar. We kept the blinds pulled. Most people who hung out in the bar during the day liked it that way. Made them think it was okay to drink their day away. We didn't have many daytime patrons, but a couple regulars frequented on a daily basis.

"Well, will you look at that?" Derrick said as he leaned over the bar to get a closer look.

Lena grinned and turned back around. "What do you think?"

"I think it's awesome," Derrick said.

Brodie walked up beside her. "Nice, is that

significant to something? Other than the guitar I mean, the wings?"

She turned back around to face everyone. "Yeah. Um … I'm single now, which means I'm free, and I can play the guitar whenever I damn well please." She'd beamed when she said that last part. I knew how much it meant to her to feel secure enough to say it too.

Brodie looked at me, nodded slowly. "Congratulations," he said softly directed toward me.

"Lena?" The male voice coming from across the bar shocked me, since no one in this town new Lena's real name except for Brodie and me.

Lena turned around. "Oh my, God!" she gasped and wrapped her arms around the guy's slim torso as he hugged her back. I wanted to know who the heck he was and why he had Lena in a tight bear hug.

"Woman, it is good to see your bright face again, finally. What a fucking relief. I've been so worried."

They finally stopped groping each other, and Lena turned toward the rest of us. "Jackson, this is Wesley, um … Weezer, my friend from Medford. Weezer, this is Jackson, his brother Brodie, and that's Derrick behind the bar. How did you find me?"

"Long story, but it was Gabby. What did you do to your hair? I almost didn't recognize you. I like it. And I see you added something else too. I like the tat."

"It stings a little still. I just got it this morning."

I had to admit I'd been relieved to find out whom this guy was. Lena had mentioned him more than once.

"How did Gabby know where I was?" she asked, a twinge of panic evident in her voice. I knew from what Lena had told me that Gabby was short for their mutual friend Gabriella, who sang backup with the band she used to play with.

"Can we go sit and talk in private?" Weezer asked.

"Yeah. Um … Jackson knows everything. I don't have any secrets from him."

Weezer raised an eyebrow and shrugged. "Okay."

"I'll get some coffee and bring it over," Brodie offered, which surprised me. Was my brother finally accepting that Lena was here to stay? Or maybe he thought someone was here to take her away and was happy to help. I wasn't sure.

"You look good, Lena. Someone must be taking very good care of you." His eyes shot to me. "I approve," he added with a smile, which quickly turned to a frown when he turned his attention back to her. "Listen, as much as I would love this to be just a chance meeting, it's not. I've been looking for you."

"Why?"

"To warn you."

Lena tensed and pressed her lips in a tight line. "Warn me about what?"

"Troy. I wanted to come and let you know that he might know where you are. I don't know for sure. Gabby was on vacation with her boyfriend last month or so. They'd been camping around this area. I think by the lake. They'd heard about the parade and decided to check it out. She saw you. She didn't know that you'd left Troy. In fact, she didn't know anything about what had happened. I never told her since you asked me not to tell anyone. After she'd seen you, or thought she'd seen you, she ran into Troy one night and mentioned that she thought she saw you at the parade here in Turtle Lake. She said she called out to you, but you didn't stop, so she figured maybe it wasn't you after all. She'd asked Troy if you were out of town, but he didn't really confirm it, just sort of shrugged and smiled at her. She asked him how you were and if he thought you'd like some company since she hadn't seen you for a while. Then he told her you *were* out of town, visiting your brother. That's when she became suspicious. She knew you didn't have a brother. She came to me two days ago and told me."

"They're divorced now," I said with confidence.

"Well, congratulations on that, sweet thing. Troy didn't mention that to Gabby. So I'm guessing he's not too happy about it."

Brodie showed up with the coffee and sat down. I looked at him. "What are you doing?"

"I want to help."

"What?"

"You're my brother and she's your girlfriend. I want to help."

I nodded and patted him on the shoulder. "Thanks."

Weezer continued, "It only took me two days to find you, and I was speeding most of the time. I left

Medford twenty minutes after Gabby told me. That was two hours after she'd spoken to Troy."

"Let's go home," I said.

We all stood, and Lena hugged Weezer. "Thank you. You better not stick around here. If Troy does come in here looking for me and sees you, I'm afraid of what he might do, Weezer. Promise me you'll leave and go home."

"I'm leaving. I'm not going home for a while, though. I thought I'd take a little vacation of my own. My sister lives a little further south in Folsom. She had a baby boy about a month ago that I haven't seen, yet. I'm an uncle," he said smiling. "I'm going to go see my nephew. You take care of our girl," he said, looking at me.

"Congratulations, Weezer, and thanks again. You're the best."

Weezer walked out the front door. We headed toward the back. That's where I always parked. "Derrick, lock up early tonight. If anyone comes in asking for me or Lana, or Lena, tell them you never heard of us."

"Call Doc, ask him to come by and play bouncer." Derrick's eyebrows rose. "Will do, boss. Anything I should be aware of?"

"Yeah, Lena's ex is a bastard that won't take no for an answer."

"Lena? I thought her name was Lana."

"It's both, but keep that to yourself," I yelled as we hurried out the door, wishing I hadn't just screwed up her name.

Chapter 42
Lena

My body shook uncontrollably as I sat in the passenger side of Jackson's SUV. Brodie drove his truck and followed close behind us.

"Jackson."

He glanced at me briefly before focusing back on the road as we whipped around the corner. "Yeah?"

"I'm sorry," I said, the shakiness in my voice made it difficult to speak very loud.

"You have nothing to be sorry about. Everything is going to be fine. You hear me? Everything. I hope you're not upset about Brodie helping. I didn't tell him details, but he's no dummy, Lena."

"I'm not." I'd always been privy to the fact that

Brodie knew more than he was letting on; otherwise he wouldn't have been giving Jackson such a difficult time about helping me. "What are we going to do?"

"We are going to pack our bags and go on vacation too."

"Where to?"

"Have you ever been to Aspen? I hear there's still plenty of snow for skiing right now."

"We can't go to Aspen."

"Why not?"

"Well, for one, we don't have a flight reservation."

"Details."

I almost laughed. "Or money."

"I have money, and we can make arrangements for the next available flight. We can hide out at the house. Your ex doesn't know where we live."

That was true, but if he did come all the way down here to find me, he'd be sure never to leave any stone unturned. I knew my husband. Not my husband anymore, I corrected. "I can't let you use your money for this."

"Why not? I need a vacation, and Aspen sounds great right now. Can you ski?"

I shook my head.

"Well, you can take a lesson. It will be fun. I promise."

I knew what he was doing with his lighthearted attitude, trying to make me feel more secure, talking about things like there was nothing wrong, calling it a vacation when we were really just running, going to hideout. The running and hiding part didn't bother me, but dragging Jackson into my horror did. "How long do you think we can keep on running until we run out of money?" I asked.

He gave me a sideways glance and frowned. "Forever, if we have to. Forever."

Right then I knew how much I loved Jackson. I'd fallen pretty hard, but I hadn't let myself admit it until just then. I couldn't let him sacrifice everything he'd worked so hard for just to help me.

Brodie pulled into the driveway right behind us. He hurried out of the jeep and ran to the front door, Rufus on his heels, but the dog quickly made a beeline over to Jackson. Rufus was Jackson's dog through and through. "What's the plan?" Brodie asked.

"Lena and I are going to Aspen. I'm hoping to find a flight out tomorrow morning." Jackson said after we'd gotten inside and he shut the door. I walked toward the backdoor and the stairs leading to the cottage. I needed to get my stuff together. I wasn't so sure about going to Aspen, but I needed to go somewhere. Alone.

Brodie nodded in agreement without even raising an eyebrow. "I have some money saved that I can give you." I stopped in my tracks and stared at Brodie. This was what family was about, pulling together to help one another in times of crisis. Something I'd never experienced before. Unconditional love. Oh, I knew my mother loved me, and she would have protected me if she'd been able to, but that was a mother's job. To have a brother or a sister give up his hard earned cash to help was beyond my comprehension, and I suddenly had a new admiration for Brodie. I couldn't let him give up his own money though.

"No!" I shouted. "I can't let you do that. Either of you."

I raced up the steps taking two at a time. Rufus barked behind me. Jackson must have told him to follow me. I headed for the closet. I pulled out all the clothes, including a dress that Leslie and I had found one day when she'd invited me along to go shopping in Fall River. It was white and covered with roses, definitely a springtime dress. I hadn't worn it yet. I wondered how much time we actually had until Troy found me. I wanted a chance to let Jackson see the dress. See me in something other than raggedy old jeans. I decided if I wore a jacket I could travel in a dress just as well as pants, so I put it on. I had no intentions of going to Aspen or anywhere with Jackson. I needed to go alone, but I wanted us to have just one last wonderful evening together, even if it had to be a short one. Jackson was right. Troy didn't know where we lived, so we were safe. For now.

Chapter 43
Jackson

There was really nothing for Brodie to do, so he went back to the bar to check on things there. He'd called in earlier and spoke to Doc, and to my relief, nobody had come in asking about Lena or Lana. So I relaxed a bit, but didn't want to let my guard down too much.

I needed to get some stuff out of storage; some snow clothes, gloves and other accessories like a hat and pants. I was looking forward to teaching Lena how to ski. I decided I'd go later after Brodie came home. I didn't want to leave her alone.

When she came in through the back door, I did a double take. I thought my eyes were playing tricks on me as she walked through the door in a dress. The way the descending sun radiated around her body made her glow like the angel I knew she was. "Wow. You look beautiful."

"Thank you."

"You're welcome, but why are you wearing a dress? I thought you were packing for our trip."

"I packed. We won't be leaving until tomorrow, right?"

I nodded.

"Well, I thought it would be nice to make tonight special. I haven't had a chance to wear this yet."

"Lena, you'll have plenty of chances to wear it later."

"But we're going someplace where it snows. And this isn't exactly a cold whether outfit."

"Well, you do look beautiful. Are you cold?" I asked, rubbing my hands up her bare arms.

"Maybe just a little. But I have you to keep me warm."

"That you do. That you do." I kissed her softly. Her hands roamed over my back and up into my hair. I loved having her fingers tangled in my hair. I decided right then never to cut it short again. I kissed my way down her neck, licking and kissing at her pulse. My own heart pounded against my chest. This dress wasn't going to stay on very long I thought as I snaked my hand up her warm bare thigh. Two minutes later, we were back in my room rolling around on the bed. The dress in a heap on the floor and all thoughts of that creep of an ex looking for her blurred away.

"My dress is all wrinkled now," Lena complained, picking it up and stepping back into it.

"Sorry, I lost control," I said, pulling my jeans back up.

She smiled, her lips still swollen from my kisses. I rubbed my chin, realizing I hadn't shaved that morning. I didn't have the toughest beard, but still, the little stubbles I did have managed to make her face a bit pink around her mouth. "I should have shaved this morning."

She touched her fingers to my lips and stepped into me. "I didn't notice."

"I think your lips did. Your mouth is all puffy. I'll go shave now so when I kiss you later tonight I'll be all smooth."

"Hmmm … I'm looking forward to that."

"My smoothness or my kisses?

"Your kisses. Your stubbles don't bother me. Nothing bothers me when you're kissing me." She slipped her arms around my neck and shimmied her body against mine.

"Woman, you better step back and stop talking that way, or I'm gonna to have to remove your dress again."

She giggled. "Is that a promise or a threat?"

My cell phone rang as Brodie's name showed up on the screen. "Ugh. It's Brodie. I better answer it." I pushed the button and walked into the bathroom to start shaving while I talked. "Yeah, we'll be leaving in the morning," I said into the phone as Lena headed toward the door. "Don't go anywhere," I said to her and she rolled her eyes and put her hands on her hips. I told Brodie to hold on and turned to Lena. "Sweetheart, I don't want to sound like a dominating prick, but I need you to stay safe. I'd never forgive myself if something happened to you."

"I'm just going to the kitchen."

Chapter 44
Lena

I strolled into the kitchen, now very hungry after rolling around in the bedroom for an hour. I glanced around and something was missing. With all the excitement, I'd left the flowers in the SUV. I raced outside to get them so I could place them in some water. I hoped they hadn't wilted from being in the car all day. I opened the car door, and there they were on the floor on the passenger's side, right where I'd left them. I picked them up, and one fell out onto the seat. I picked it up and held it to my nose, inhaling its sweet aroma.

As I turned to head back up the stairs, a hand covered my mouth as Troy whispered into my ear. "Lena, baby, it's been a long time."

I gasped into his hand and dropped the bouquet of roses on the ground. I held onto the loose one. I didn't know why, other than something in the back of my mind told me I should, that I might need it or something.

"Don't make a sound, Lena. This isn't just a piece of metal sticking into your side." My eyes flicked down to the pistol digging into my ribs, hoping I didn't really see what my skin felt. Troy shoved me toward the side yard, back toward the cottage. All the blinds were down on the windows on this side of the house, so I didn't think Jackson would see what was going on. I prayed that Jackson would realize I went outside. I should have said something, but I knew he would jump up and offer to fetch the flowers himself, and I really just needed some fresh air. Stupid. I should have trusted my instincts and realized Troy would find me without the help of anyone in that bar.

"I bet you thought you'd killed me, huh, Lena. Well, let me tell you, you nearly did." He laughed, and his familiar hot, boozy breath assaulted my ear.

"Fuck, Lena, you were never any good at finishing things. You made me have to *lie* to the doctor, though." He said the word "lie" through clenched teeth, as if it were poison to utter the forbidden word. "I had to tell the doctor I punctured my stomach in the garage while trying to hang a new garage door opener. I told her that the whole thing snapped, and the steel rod flew down straight into my stomach just inches from doing any major damage, just like the pathetic little knife you shoved into my gut. Of course, I had to make the wound you inflicted look jagged, which hurt like a son of a fucking bitch. Lucky for me, you didn't thrust that knife in a bit further or I would be a dead man. I'd waited a couple hours before actually going into the emergency room. Hell, I needed to sober up a little first. Almost considered skipping the stitches entirely, but when I couldn't get the bleeding to stop after shoving the damn steel in my gut making the wound worse, and more jagged, I'd had no choice. That was your fault. I suppose the extra irritant to the wound with the metal rod didn't help much, since the fucking doctor almost didn't believe my story anyway, and nearly called the cops. I had to do some fancy sweet-talking to convince her I was on the up and up. Good thing the doc was a woman, I've always been able to sweet talk women you know.

"And on top of that, you bitch, I'd torn my shirt and got it all stained with blood trying to make it look like an accident. I had to tear the shirt, and that pissed me off. Work shirts aren't cheap, so you're gonna pay for that too."

He kept shoving me forward, the gun pressed firmly against my side and his hand still covered my mouth. We made our way past my car and snuck around the side of the garage. Too bad I didn't have my keys. I could have sounded the alarm on the car. The woods were about a hundred yards away, and I had the feeling that was where he was taking me. He must have left his car somewhere down the road and hiked in through the woods. My hand was still clasped around the stem of the rose. I didn't feel any thorns that I could use to scratch his face. Since when did roses come without thorns? Of course, that would have only made him more deranged, and God, I didn't want to do that. He was sick. I knew that now.

"It took me some time to recover from that, Lena. I lost time at work, and damn it, bitch, you made me miss Taco Tuesday at the bar that night. You know I really thought I could trust you," He continued his rant through a clenched jaw, "I really thought you'd be back at home, sitting on the couch waiting for me to return from the fucking emergency room. When you weren't there, I threw my keys against the wall, made a big gash in the plaster too. Landlord's gonna want some money for that." Troy was rambling now as if him telling me all this would somehow make it all better. "I'd had to get drunk all over again just to dull the pain from the stabbing. I musta guzzled several beers down in one gulp. Woke up to find all the empties in the sink, broken. You're gonna clean them up, 'cause I left them for you."

I was right; we were heading into the woods behind the garage. As we made our way into the forest, I tripped over a log and almost fell. Troy was strong though, and he managed to hold me up without moving his hand away from my face. "Watch where you're stepping," he growled. Troy didn't bother with the trail, and there was no way to know what sort of foliage or shrubbery we'd be running into until we were right on top of it because I couldn't move my head very well to see with his hand covering my mouth and holding my head still that way. Branches and thorns scraped my legs as we hurried past them.

"I figured you'd run over to one of those druggy friends you used to hang out with when I'd first met you. What was her name? Oh yeah ... Gabby, Gabriella D something or other, and what was that jerk's name? Geezer? No, Weezer. Weezer Storm. Well, hold on, Weezer my man, looks like Daddy's found his girl, and just as soon as I get my Lena home, we'll need to pay good ol' Weezer a visit," he muttered as though Weezer was walking along with us. "Oh, and you can thank your friend, Gabby for tipping me off about where you've been hiding. Why here for fuck's sake, anyway?"

I heard Rufus bark not so very far from us, and hoped Troy wouldn't realize he was chasing us. If Rufus was close then I knew Jackson was too. and I hoped to God they didn't find us because Troy had a gun, and I didn't want Jackson or Rufus to get hurt.

As Rufus' bark got closer, Troy's grip tightened on my mouth. "It sounds like that asswipe you've been staying with is following us. Adultery is a sin, Lena. I thought I could trust you." Apparently, the final divorce papers didn't mean anything to Troy. He was refusing to recognize the fact that we were no longer married. "You better hope he doesn't get any closer. I have no problem silencing that thing or the adulterer he belongs to."

Troy's arm became tighter and tighter around my head, and his hand smashed against my mouth. I considered biting his palm, but the way he had it positioned made it impossible, plus with the gun sticking into my ribs, I thought it best not to provoke him. Panic seared through my mind as I tried to suck in some air. His fingers covered my mouth, but also blocked all the air from my nostrils. I was feeling faint, and my body went limp as my consciousness drifted away. Rufus' barking became a muffled sound in the distance, and Troy swore under his breath, "You stone-cold, frigid bitch. I can't carry you all the way to the fucking tru…"

Chapter 45
Jackson

I'd called out to Lena to ask her what she'd like to eat, and when she didn't answer, I went looking for her. It didn't take long to realize she was nowhere inside the house, and I'd searched every room. I ran outside and saw the car door open, the bouquet of roses scattered on the ground. I quickly scanned the front yard before I ran up the stairs to the cottage. I didn't think she was up there, but I hoped. When I reached the top step, I saw Lena and some guy, who I realized must be her son of a bitch ex, heading into the woods. He had his arm gripped around her neck and his hand covering her mouth. I opened my mouth to yell when I saw the gun he had stuck into her back. I swallowed the urge to shout out for fear he would shoot her.

I ran down the stairs. "Rufus stay," I demanded, but I think Rufus figured out what was happening, and for the first time in his life, he didn't listen to me and took off toward the woods.

I didn't see them anywhere, but Rufus charged ahead, and I was grateful that he hadn't stayed when I told him to. I lost sight of him and called out, but he continued at full speed. I was surprised, considering he was always so lazy, but I couldn't stop him. Rufus had fallen in love with Lena, just like me, and he was determined to save her.

I didn't really know what I was going to do when I caught up to them. The guy had a gun. I had nothing but my hands. I'd have to sneak up on him, but Rufus had his own agenda, and it wasn't about being sneaky. I lost track of him when he turned toward the left and his barking became a consistent howl before turning into a growl and two shots rang out. The sound echoed through the trees, and my heart leapt into my throat. My God, had he shot Lena? Or did he shoot Rufus? Or both?

I ran as fast as I could, and when I caught sight of the guy standing in a small clearing, I stopped and tiptoed to the edge, crouched down and peered through the bushes. Oh no, Lena's body lay to his right, one of the roses clutched in her hand, and Troy stood over my dog's limp body, blood oozing from his side making his dark mange look wet. I needed a plan. He still had a gun, so I figured my best approach would be from behind. He was a big guy. I couldn't tell how tall he was, he looked to be my height, but clearly had twenty pounds on me. I didn't know if I could take him, but I had to try. He stood with his back to me, the gun in his right hand pointed at the ground.

"Fucking dog! Who's dog is this Lena?" he asked aloud.

She didn't respond. I didn't know if she was alive or not. "Please, God, please let her be alive. Let them both stay alive."

Blood dripped from the guys left forearm, and I realized Rufus must have bitten him. "Fucking dog!" he yelled again, and kicked Rufus in the gut. Rufus whimpered, unable to defend himself anymore, and rage took over every cautious bone in my body as I jumped up and ran toward the guy, wrapping my arms around his body and shoving him to the ground. I didn't know if he still held the gun or not, but I turned him over and slugged him in the jaw. The guy hit back, and caught me in the cheek as he shoved me off of him. We scrambled to our feet, but I was a bit quicker, and laid another set of knuckles into his face. The gun nowhere in sight, I gained my courage and charged him, taking us both to the ground again. We wrestled in the dirt until I managed to get on top, and I hit him in the jaw again with my right hand, then again with my left. I kept hitting him and hitting him until Lena shouted, "That's enough!" but I didn't pay any attention. "Jackson! That's enough. He's out cold. Stop! You're gonna kill him." Lena's hands were on my shoulders urging me off of him.

I stopped hitting him and got up, and Lena embraced me. Her face soaked from tears, horror on her face when she saw Rufus. "Rufus!" she gasped. We hurried to Rufus and knelt beside him. His breathing was shallow, but he was still alive. "Sorry boy, I'm so sorry. We'll get you fixed up."

"So brave," Lena said, stroking Rufus' head as he looked up at her. His eyes turned glassy and then closed.

"Let's get out of here," I said. But I only got Rufus up about an inch off the ground when Troy's fist pounded into the side of my head, knocking me backwards with Rufus on top of me. I managed to place my dog back on the ground without dropping him. Troy charged at me, pinning me to the ground, punching me again in the jaw. Then his fist jammed into my left eye, his legs straddled my torso, and the twenty pounds I estimated felt like fifty as his hands went around my throat.

"She belongs to me," he said through clenched teeth, and continued choking me. I tried to pry his fingers from my neck, but with all his weight and his advantaged position over me, I couldn't budge them. I used every ounce of strength I had to pry his hands from my throat. Somewhere deep down inside of me I saw this guy punching Lena over and over again if I didn't get free of him. I don't know where the strength came from, but I fisted my right hand, forcing it up and connecting with Troy's mouth. He loosened his grip around my throat, and I shoved him off me. I rolled over, coughing and sputtering, trying to catch my breath.

Before I had a chance to stand up, Troy was on me again. This time, a very large rock in this hand ready to pound into my head. "She's my wife!" he shouted, spitting blood into my face.

"Not anymore!" Lena shouted, and he glanced at her. "I hate you, Troy Harrington," she cried, and once again the forest filled with the deadly sound of gunfire.

The bullet hit Troy smack dab in the middle of his chest, blood trickled out and dripped onto my face, adding to the muck he'd already spit at me as his body stopped moving above mine. Maybe two or three seconds later he collapsed on top of me, his blood soaking my shirt.

Lena stood shaking, and Brodie ran into the small clearing and over to her. "He was choking him. He was killing Jackson. I had to. I had to shoot him."

"I know," my brother soothed, taking the gun from her hands. "I know. It's over now, Lena. It's all over."

I managed to get on my knees as she ran to me, wrapping her arms around me, almost making me tumble backwards again. "I love you, Jackson," she sobbed into my neck. "I love you so much."

I held her, rocking back and forth.

"Sorry I didn't get here any sooner," Brodie said. "When I got home from the bar, it wasn't until I heard the gun shots that I realized something was wrong. I ran out here as fast as I could. Just in time to see …" He didn't say what he saw, but we both knew what he saw.

Chapter 46
Lena

"You were very brave, too," I whispered into Jackson's ear, leaning my head on his shoulder. I didn't know if he smiled or not. It didn't matter. I sat between him and Brodie in the veterinary emergency waiting room. They were operating on Rufus. Poor sweet, brave Rufus had lost so much blood; the doctor didn't seem too hopeful about the outcome, and warned us to be prepared for the worst. Jackson turned into me and buried his face against my shoulder. I held on to him, unable to contain my own tears as I closed my eyes, praying silently that Rufus would make it.

I don't know how long we waited. It felt like hours, but every time Jackson asked Brodie what time it was, each time, only about ten minutes had passed. Brodie's phone rang, and he got up, speaking into it as he walked a little bit away. Jackson stayed with me, his elbows resting on his knees, his face in his hands. I had my arm around his back, and I rubbed my hand gently up and down. I figured it was the police on the phone. I dreaded to hear what they were saying. I had just killed Troy. I really killed him this time. Brodie had called the police on our way to the vet's, telling them what happened. Neither Jackson nor I could utter a word, our thoughts on Rufus the entire ride.

A few minutes later, Brodie sat down beside me. "The cops located Troy's body. They're going to want to talk to all of us."

Jackson nodded and wiped his face with the palms of his hands.

"They know it was self-defense. It'll be okay," Brodie said. "Brad Grayson is a friend of ours, and was a good friend of our uncle's. He's leading the investigation. He said he'd wait until after we get Rufus home before he comes over."

"*If* we take him home," Jackson said quietly.

"The bullet went into his right hip just above his leg," Jackson explained to Derrick who'd been tending to the bar almost exclusively by himself while Brodie and Jackson spent most of their time with Rufus at the veterinary hospital, and then a couple days at home.

Even though Rufus was, by all accounts, Jackson's dog, Brodie loved him just as much. Rufus lay on a thick burly blanket in the corner of the room, gnawing on the largest rawhide bone I'd ever seen. His leg and hip remained bandaged, and he would need to stay off it for a few days, which meant he needed to be carried everywhere. Brodie rigged up this cute little transport using some old wagon wheels and a rug covered board he'd found in the shed to help during potty times. The doctor sounded very positive that Rufus would gain full use of his leg in no time. I couldn't have been more relieved. To think that I had anything to do with the possible harming of such a wonderful dog sickened me. It sickened me to know what a monster I had been married to.

Jackson put his arm around me and pulled me against him, almost as if he sensed my thoughts. He stopped hiding his affections for me from Brodie, not that he'd managed to do that in the first place. Brodie always knew.

The comforting feel of Jackson's body against mine soothed me. I never would have made it through the past couple of nights if Jackson hadn't spent the nights sleeping next to me. I'd woken up three separate times screaming. The visions of Troy's face as his words taunted me Saying, "She belongs to me." Demanding it. Those were Troy's last words before *I'd* killed him. Right after I'd stopped Jackson from doing the deed. I'm glad though. I didn't want Jackson to carry that guilt around for the rest of his life; the guilt of killing another human being, even if it was to stop him from killing someone else.

The door to the bar opened, letting in a path of brightness and warmth from the sun, which was also blinding, making it difficult to see who was entering until the door closed tight again.

"Lena?"

I turned to see Gabby, my friend from the band and the girl who'd apparently seen me at the parade and had unintentionally revealed my whereabouts.

Chapter 47
Jackson

Lena rushed to hug the girl who'd just entered the bar as we stood by waiting to see who she was.

"Oh, my, God! Lena, are you all right? I had to come and see you. Weezer called and told me what a mess I'd made of everything. I'm so sorry."

"Gabby, it's okay. How were you to know? I never told you about the kind of person Troy was."

"Well, I had my suspicions. How could I not? You dropped out of the band and never wanted to come out anymore. I should have been a better friend."

"You were the perfect friend. I didn't want you or anyone involved." Lena grabbed the girl by the arm and walked her over to us. "Jackson, Brodie, this is my friend Gabriella, Gabby for short."

Gabby smiled and tucked a loose strand of her long dark hair that hung down to her slim waist behind her ear. The slight curl in the strands made it look thick and luxurious. My brother elbowed me, grinning, and I instantly knew what he was thinking.

"Hey," she said, shaking my hand and then Brodie's.

"Any friend of Lena's is a friend of ours." Brodie gave her his best, I'm-available-to-show-you-the-town-anytime, smile.

"She sings backup with Weezer's band," Lena added, proudly. "She's very good."

"Not anymore," she said.

"What? Why?"

"Weezer decided to stay in southern California to be closer to his sister. He said he needed his family. His sister was all he had left. The band fell apart without him."

"Oh, so how long will you be here?"

"Not too long, but I just got here. I haven't even made arrangements yet. I'm on my way to San Diego. I'm moving there. I am looking for a change now that the band split up, but I wanted to make sure you were okay first. Oh, God, Lena, I can't believe it was me who gave you away to that creep. I wish I'd known."

I decided to do the brotherly thing, for Brodie's sake. "You're welcome to stay with us for a few nights." Brodie elbowed me in the arm again, but managed to keep his face placid. I knew what was going through his mind though. My brother may have wanted to show this girl the town, but he sure as hell didn't like the idea of his lifestyle being put in jeopardy. Having a beautiful girl in the house that he wanted to get to know better meant he'd need to keep his "other lady associates" to a minimum during her stay.

"Really?" Lena said. Neither of the ladies noticed Brodie's sudden change in moods.

"Well, it is my brother's house. What do you say, Brodie?"

He cleared his throat. "Well, sure." He managed without a hitch. This was going to be interesting. Who knows, maybe Brodie's demons were beginning to fade away.

Lena had made an awesome lasagna for dinner, being the perfect hostess for her friend. Brodie actually helped make Gabby's stay very comfortable, setting her up in the spare bedroom for the next few nights. Giving her extra pillows and showing her around the house, making sure she had everything she needed. Gabby, it seemed, promised to be quite different from the girls Brodie usually spent time with, and she made it quite clear from the beginning that she wasn't going to be the easy conquer he was used to. He had his work cut out for him that's for sure. I wondered if he would just leave, and find some other girl to give his attention to for the next few days, or if he'd rise to the challenge, and put all of his efforts into Gabby. She was a knockout, and just the type he liked, but Brodie had his own demons to deal with. I hoped to God he'd come to terms with them some day.

Lena watched them sitting on the sofa perusing some of the music sheets that were scattered over the coffee table. Gabby giggled at something Brodie said, and Lena shrugged.

We said goodnight to Gabby leaving her in the company of my brother. Lena was a little reluctant at first to leave Gabby alone with Brodie, and I had to remind her that Gabby was a big girl. She seemed very capable of handling herself with a wolf like Brodie. Brodie might try to seduce her, but he knew what the word "no" meant.

"Come with me, baby," I tugged Lena into my bedroom. *Our* bedroom I corrected. I needed some alone time with her lovely body. With all the worrying about Rufus I'd forgotten about how she must be feeling about killing Troy. And besides, she looked too good in the new dress she'd purchased today when she'd gone shopping with Gabby during their "girl time" they'd insisted on having. I needed to see if she had anything exiting on underneath. I pulled her against me as we entered the room. "I love you, Lena, you know that? I think I fell for you the moment you walked in my bar."

She smiled. "Good, because I'm not going

anywhere. I happen to love you too."

I flipped the switch on the wall that illuminated a small bedside lamp, giving the room a soft glow, light enough to see her beautiful eyes sparkle, but dark enough to keep a hint of mystery as we explored each other's bodies. "You saved me," I whispered against her neck. "Thank you." Those two words of thanks didn't seem to be nearly enough. I didn't think there were enough words in the universe to express my undying thanks to her. I needed her to know how much I admired what she'd done for me. It had taken a great amount of courage to pull that trigger. She wrapped her arms around my neck and kissed my lips. Then she kissed the corner of my mouth, then the other side, making her way down my neck to my chest. She shoved the cotton material of my unbuttoned shirt aside and laid little kisses down to my stomach. I shuddered with excitement, almost forgetting what I wanted to say to her. I took her face in my hands and brought her lips back to mine. I kissed her slowly, tenderly, before pulling away. "Lena, I want you to know how much I admire the strength it took for you to do what you did for me. You saved me, baby. Do you get it?"

"Yes, I saved you, but you saved me first, Jackson Beaumont. And I will never forget that."

"Sweetheart, you couldn't have been saved if you hadn't wanted to be. It had to come from here," I pointed to her head, "and from here." I rested the palm of my hand in the center of her chest. "You left him on your own. I was merely a stepping-stone to your recovery. You're a strong, beautiful, independent woman, Lena. Don't ever forget that."

Chapter 48
Lena

Yeah...

I understood what Jackson meant, though I was having trouble accepting it. A huge part of me still felt that vulnerability. The insecurity weaved its way through my brain cells, toxic and demoralizing. I looked at my hands, now tainted with murder. Murder of a sick man, but still *I* killed him. The police were very accepting and understanding of what happened. Having Brodie as my witness helped tremendously and I wouldn't be facing any charges, none with the law that is. I only had my own demons to fight and the nightmares that came with them.

"I hate what I did, killing Troy," I admitted finally. "I hate Troy even more for making me do it, but at the same time, I'm glad I was able to save you in the process." I looked down at Jackson's hands that held mine, only because I wasn't sure I could look at his face without tears. Even though the police weren't pinning murder on me … God, would I ever be over the guilt of taking another human being's life? I knew I was to blame for everything. I'd let that relationship with Troy happen. I was the one who had to take the blame for it. Troy had been a sick man. Deep down I knew that, but I wished I could have helped him receive some sort of treatment for his illness. And deep down I also knew that men like Troy existed in many homes, and there were many women just like me. Some still in trouble. Some, the lucky ones like me, got out.

"You have to forgive yourself, Lena. In order to move on, you have to. You're the only one holding any of this against you. You didn't do anything wrong, sweetheart. Sometimes it's harder to forgive yourself and let go, but you have to try."

I braved a look and studied Jackson now. I knew I didn't need to say these words to him. I knew he understood. I don't know how, but he did. I wasn't saying them for him though. "I will never let another man do to me what Troy did."

"That's my girl," he said.

I smiled at the "my girl" reference. I liked being Jackson's girl, knowing he'd never keep me from my dreams. Hell, his were almost identical to mine. He skimmed his finger down my bare arm. The tickling sensation made me smile. Troy had never touched me that way, not even in the beginning. Oh, he wasn't violent at first, just not as tender, but that was a time in the past, a time when I didn't know tender.

"I still have some fears, and I know I need to overcome them."

"I can help with that." His smile was soft, reassuring and oh so damn sexy.

There was one particular fear that I wanted to tackle, and I didn't want to approach it like a timid wounded rabbit. I hesitated at first, not sure how Jackson would respond. I'd never been able to play the sexy vixen. Troy had been the only man I'd ever been with. Playing a role like that would have sent him into a jealous rage of swearing and accusations that I'd been with someone else. Accusing me of liking rough sex and he'd be sure to show me his way of what rough meant. No, I didn't need that kind of rough sex. But I did want some intensity. The kind I'd only been able to read about in books. The comfort I received from Jackson gave me the courage to move in, take what I wanted. I took a step closer to him. His shirt was unbuttoned, hanging loosely over his pants. I made tiny circles on his chest with my finger, and he slipped his arm around my waist. Even though the thought of being possessed the way I thought I would like frightened me, I wanted it more than anything with Jackson. Deep in my mind, I knew it was a different kind of possession, and he wouldn't hurt me. I'd seen movies, read books, I could do this.

I kept my voice low and as sexy as I thought possible. "Well, you know, I have this fear of being overpowered by a man." I bit my bottom lip and waited for his response.

"Yes, I know," he returned with just the right amount of sexy smoothness to make me almost forget what I was doing, or what I wanted to do.

I continued skimming my fingertips lightly over his chest. "Particularly in …" I looked around the room we stood in. "…in the bedroom."

"Like I said, I can help with that."

"I think I'd like that," I said and nipped at his chin.

"I've heard that the best way to tackle your fears is to experience them first hand. Throw yourself into them so to speak."

"Is that right?"

"Yeah." He took a step closer to me, then another, pinning me between him and the wall. Our bodies pressed firmly together, and he kept his face an inch above mine. With his finger, he tilted my chin up and covered my mouth with his. He didn't hurt me, but I gasped into his mouth as he kissed me, hard and demanding. His hand fisted in my hair, my blonde locks, and I had a fleeting thought that maybe I should return them back to their dark auburn color, but just as quickly as that idea entered my head, it disappeared with the taste of Jackson's tongue exploring my mouth, removing everything but him from my mind. His hand slid down my side and back up my skirt. His fingers tugged at my panties, yanking them down to my knees. As Jackson moved his thumb around in little circles, he slipped a couple fingers inside me. I had to close my eyes as the sensation took hold. Thunder roared in my head, and he kissed the spot under my ear, sucking just a little before spreading more kisses down my neck toward the scoop of my dress, where a hint of cleavage peaked out.. His fingers skimmed down my thigh and wetness coated my skin. I smiled. A little bit of me proclaiming my independence as my body accepted the freedom of this new person I was becoming.

Continue reading for a sneak peek at

Book 2 of The Beaumont Brothers, Brodie's story

Chapter 1

Brodie

The buzz coming from under my pillow pounded between my ears like thunder. I'd set my phone on vibrate, and it was determined to ruin a perfect slumbering morning. I stuck my hand under the cushion attempting to silence it, but only managed to knock the offending instrument onto the floor.

The girl beside me pulled herself into a cute little ball with her knees hugging her chest, and her adorable little behind shoved against my cock. She moaned something about it still being dark outside. No shit. I frowned, and rolling over reached for my phone unfortunately catching a glimpse at the digital clock on the nightstand in the process. A glaring red four-fifty-nine assaulted my eyes with brilliance that even Einstein would have been shocked by. The brightness made it impossible to determine who in God's name was sending me a text so early in the morning.

I let the phone slip from my fingers to the floor without bothering to read the message. There was nothing in this world so important at five o' fucking clock in the morning that couldn't wait. I rolled back toward the hottie. "Sorry, baby," I whispered into her neck, and showered her with little kisses there. Wishing I could remember her name. Casandra, Clarista, Carry? It was one of those C names or was it K? No matter. Normally, I was pretty good with names. I'd never once called a woman the wrong name, but this girl had such an uncommon, yet so close to common name I'd had trouble all night long, and had to resort to calling her baby or sweetheart. I hated using those terms of endearment because none of the girls I'd been hooking up with lately were someone I'd like to think of as endearing. "Go back to sleep," I said, sort more of an order to myself than to her.

When she scooted back against me, moving her hips the way she did, she all of a sudden seemed very endearing to me. I rocked with her, closing my eyes, shutting out the visions of the bedroom I was in with its dark purple wall and massive black and white picture of a nude couple embracing on the adjacent pale pink wall. Lacy, pale pink curtains hung in the window. Not my room. This was a commonality for me recently, waking up to find myself in unfamiliar, feminine surroundings, since privacy at home had become an issue. That explained the bright digital clock beside the bed— not something I would ever own.

Cassandra, Clarista, Castalia, or whatever the fuck her name was, let out a sexy moan before turning around and wrapping her hands around me. Stroking and squeezing oh so firmly just enough to make a guy not only forget where he was, but not care. God, it felt so good, but not as good as when her tongue slid over the tip right before taking me in her mouth.

I must admit, my breath hitched as the tip of my cock hit the back of her throat, and I caught the slight gagging sound she made. "Oh, baby. That feels so good." Actually, this Cassandra or whatever, was a bit mediocre in this particular department, but I wasn't about to complain. A poor attempt at a blowjob was better than none at all in my book.

This was my life. I wasn't complaining. Nope, not at all. Today was starting off much like any other day lately; lazy, with a little romping between the sheets. It got my blood running, and today I needed to be on my game. Today, or tonight rather, was my brother's bachelor party, and I was hosting it.

Buzzzzzzzz.

My phone again. "Hey, baby. Give me a minute will ya?" I groaned, pulling myself out from the soft sucking and into the cold air. Shit. What was wrong with me? I leaned over the edge of the bed and picked up my phone. This time I read the message. Only it wasn't a message. It was an alert I'd set on my phone as a reminder. *Pick up Gabby from airport.* My brother's soon to be bride's maid of honor—and a major pain in my side—was flying in this morning at six-twenty, and I'd been volunteered by Jackson to pick her up. Thanks a whole hell of a lot.

"Fuck."

"What's the matter, Brodie?" she asked, licking her lips and grabbing for me like she'd just had her favorite lollypop taken away.

"I gotta go."

"What? Why?"

"Sorry, baby." God, what was her name? "I promised to pick up a friend from the airport." Friend was a huge stretch of the English vocabulary when it came to Gabby. Gabriella Demers was not my friend in any sense of the word. In fact, she hated me.

The last time I saw Gabby, which was about six months ago when she'd spent a few nights in my house while visiting with Lena, she'd told me to go bungie jumping from a bridge without the bungie

273

cord. Ouch. All I'd done to deserve that nice suggestion was tried my damnedest to show the woman a good time. Of course, my idea of a good time and hers were completely different, which I found out the second my lips brushed gently against hers and my hand strategically covered her left breast. She'd shoved me away so fast my poor lips never got the chance to make even a hint of a memory of hers. Right before she told me to go jump off the bridge, she'd slapped me and said I wasn't her type. It was when I insisted that I was, that she got nasty about it. Pffft. I was every woman's type. But hey, I copped a clue right away and back off the minute she shoved me away, she didn't need to make an imprint of her hand on my face. There was something disturbing about that chick.

I shook the memory away and grabbed the waist of the one I was with, pulling her back against me. "I wish I could stay, baby, but I did promise my brother."

"Can we hook up again tonight?" she asked.

"Sorry, no can do. Got a bachelor party to host." Glad for once I had a bona fide excuse at the tip of my tongue.

"Aw. What about tomorrow night? I'll only be in town for another couple of days." Relationships just the way I liked them. Short and noncommittal. "We could have a replay of last night, maybe even make a movie so I have something to remember you by."

Make a movie? No way. I had a fine physique and all, and I may be promiscuous, very free with my organs, some might even say I'm a man slut, but I didn't need my ass in a starring role plastered all over the internet. "Love to, except I have commitments this weekend." Besides, I'd never spent the night with the same woman more than twice, and this one was barely worth the one I'd already spent.

I quickly pulled up my pants and shrugged into my shirt. I pulled on my boots and grabbed my phone, and as I headed for the door she purred out. "Call me?"

"Sure, baby." I lied as I shut the door, and deleted her number from my phone. I never saved them, and I never answered my phone when the number came up without a name attached.

Resources for victims of Domestic Violence
Know that you are not alone.

Joyful Heart Foundation
http://www.joyfulheartfoundation.org/

Helpguide.org
http://www.helpguide.org/images/global/header.jpg

NO MORE
http://nomore.org/

California Partnership to End Domestic Violence
http://www.cpedv.org/
1-800-524-4765

Or contact the National Domestic Violence 24 hour
hotline at 1-800-799-SAFE(7233)

Keep reading for a sneak peak at Allusive Aftershock, a
young adult contemporary available in digital, print and audio.
Formats.

Allusive Aftershock

Chapter 1

Adela

An enormous amount of shaking jerked me awake.

My freaking bed was bouncing underneath me. A deep growl from somewhere below rose to a violent rumbling, rocking me and everything else around in my bedroom. I bolted up in my bed not really fully awake enough to comprehend exactly what was going on. My eyes darted to the swaying floor lamp threatening to tumble over in the corner. For a moment, I sat frozen, unable to move as I watched my silver jewelry box slide off my dresser and crash to the floor. Bracelets, earrings, and necklaces scattered over the hardwood surface.

Shoving the covers aside, I jumped out of bed and tripped over the blankets hanging from the side of the mattress, falling on my hands and knees in my haste to get to my parents' room. I picked my wobbly self up and took off toward their doorway, colliding with my dad. We held on to one another to steady ourselves from the swaying movement of the rumbling house.

My little sister screeched from down the hall, "What's happening, what's happening?!" I glanced toward the sound of her piercing squeal, which only fueled the deafening roar with more hysteria. "Go to your mother." My dad shoved me in the direction of their king-sized bed as he took off toward the room my four-year-old sister and brother shared.

I jumped into my mom's out-stretched arms and we huddled together in the center of the bed. For a split second I thought, *are we at war?* It may have been a stupid notion, but you'd be surprised at what flips through your mind in the middle of a disaster. I didn't know what war felt like, but I was positive it had to be something this frightening.

My mom's arms wrapped tighter around my shoulders, the bed bouncing and rocking beneath us as I tried to think who might be bombing us. Because, if we were being bombed, surely that big blast of light would come at any minute and it would all be over. Somehow, through my fear I wracked my brain trying to remember which countries possessed nuclear weapons. North Korea came to mind, a topic we'd discussed at length in history class only last week.

The bedroom windows shook and rattled and I thought they would explode any second. A crashing sound came from somewhere else in the house and the earsplitting shatter of glass rang in my head. As my mom and I huddled together, I stared out the large sliding glass door leading to the swimming pool. Traces of the early morning sun made things barely visible as water sloshed around, spilling over the edge. The surrounding pavement rippled in waves.

The bedside lamp toppled over and I almost jumped out of my skin when the bulb exploded as it hit the hardwood floor. *This is it.* I was sure my life was over.

My father shouted from down the hall, "They're okay!"

My mom sighed, squeezing her arms around my body even tighter and whispering close to my ear, "It's an earthquake."

"An earthquake?" I wasn't quite sure which was worse, being blown to smithereens or swallowed by the earth as it cracked wide open. Maybe the roof would cave in and crush us to death. Not that it mattered. *Dead is dead.*

In what seemed like an eternity of seconds later, the shaking stopped.

The roaring and rumbling ceased and quiet settled around us except for my sister's whimpering and my dad's soothing voice.

The sudden stillness seemed eerie, as if it was only temporary and the shaking and rumbling would start up again any second.

My mom cupped my face in her hands and made me look in her eyes. "Are you okay, Adela?" Her voice had the uncanny ability to soothe me even in a nerve-wracking situation like this. Maybe that's why my dad called her Angel, aside from the fact that it was short for Angelica. Angelica Castielle … sort of had a solacing ring to it, I always thought.

I nodded and swiped away the uncontrollable tears rolling down my cheeks.

"Come on, let's go see the twins." We got up from the bed and walked down the hall to the twins' room. Aaron, my little brother and Ambrosia, my little sister sat on the bottom bunk; our dad between them, his big hand fluffing Aaron's hair. His broad smile lightened the situation as he glanced up at my mom and me. Aaron studied his fingers, twisting them in his red Superman blanket and Ambrosia sniffled against Dad's broad chest.

"There, it's all over now," he cooed softly and squeezed them close.

My mom took a step toward them and they jumped into her arms. I hung back, leaning against the door, too devastated at the sight of the toys and decorations that had fallen off the shelves and now lay strewn about on the floor. A picture of me and the twins my mom had made us pose for last Christmas lay face up on the floor, the glass of the frame broken into a million tiny pieces. I tried to swallow the lump in my throat. The last thing the twins needed was to see me cry.

"Look, Mommy, my fire truck ladder." Aaron's bottom lip protruded slightly, but he managed to keep his tough boyish bravado in check as he held two halves of a white plastic ladder in his hands.

"Sorry, sweetie."

"Give it here, pal. I think I can glue it." Aaron handed the two pieces of the ladder to my dad and sat back down beside him on the bed.

Dad patted Aaron on the head and stood, approached me, and placed his fingers under my chin as I lifted my eyes to his. "Okay, Dely?"

Words stuck in my throat and a sob threatened, so I only nodded.

He smiled but his eyes stayed firm and serious as he walked out of the room. I turned and ran after him. "Dad, what about the horses?" I asked, struggling to clear the sob from my voice.

"I'm gonna get dressed and check on them now."

"I want to come."

"I think your mother needs you here."

"Dad, please? Big Blue needs me. The earthquake had to scare him. He'll be so frightened. Please."

This time, his dark eyes smiled along with his mouth. "Okay, Adela. But once we see he's okay, you're back here, helping your mother."

"Okay, I promise." I sprinted to my room and stopped in the doorway, taking in the horrible sight. My favorite picture lay on the floor. I picked it up and turned it over before placing it back on the dresser. Luckily, there wasn't a scratch on it. My mom had taken it two years ago at my fifteenth birthday party. Max and I had just had a cake fight, and we smiled for the camera with our heads close together, faces smudged with chocolate frosting. I loved that picture; it represented one of the happiest times in my life. I turned to grab the pants I'd left draped over the back of the glider in the corner of my room, a habit that always invoked a threat of donation to Goodwill by my mother. On my way, I tripped over the jewelry box still sitting in the middle of the floor. I sighed at the sight, all my jewelry tangled and scattered around the floor, including the delicate heart pendant my mom had given me on my seventeenth birthday four months ago. I picked it up and put it on, stared at the other stuff on the floor, and sighed. *I'll worry about the rest of the mess later.*

I tugged up my jeans and shrugged on a long-sleeved shirt, buttoning it one-handed, grabbing an elastic band from the doorknob with the other. I didn't even bother combing my hair, just ran my fingers through the tangles, and pulled it back, looping the hair band several times around it. I snatched my jacket from the hook behind the door, pulling it on as I ran to the kitchen, grabbed an apple from the bowl filled with assorted fruit on the counter, and shoved it into my jacket pocket.

Passing the living room, I saw the mess of scattered, broken china on the floor in front of the hutch. Mom stood at the edge of the room, shaking her head. I could almost feel her anguish at the sight in front of her. With her hands clasped together, fingers folded into the soft peach Angora wool of her sweater, she crushed the collar close to her chin as if it was a security blanket; maybe it was to her. My dad had given her that sweater last Christmas and she wore it all the time.

"Sorry, Mom." I wanted to comfort her but she waved me on, not even looking at me. The china set, an heirloom from my mother's family, passed down for five generations, would have one day belonged to Ambrosia or me. Well, that decision was no longer an issue. At that moment, I realized nothing lasts forever. Particularly porcelain china.

The smell of hay mixed with horse manure assaulted my nose when I strolled into the stable no less than two minutes later. Most people cringe at that smell, but I embraced it. It meant I was near Big Blue. I walked past my dad who'd already shoveled most of the hay into the trough, and headed straight to Big Blue's stall.

"Adela, don't go in there yet. He's very skittish and might stomp on you by accident. I'm going to give Courtland Reese a call. I want him to check out Blue before you ride him. That is, if he hasn't already been solicited by another rancher around here."

"Dad, seriously? Courtland Reese? Come on. I know Big Blue better than anyone. I can handle him, can't I, big boy?" I said, as I got closer to my horse.

Courtland Reese was the boy everyone at school hated and made fun of because of his freakish connection to animals. Well, Max hated him, mostly. Everyone else just went along with whatever Max said.

I reached over the gate and placed my hand on Blue's head and he reared back, flaring his nostrils as if he didn't know me. I recoiled in shock.

No. Big Blue can't do this. He's my baby. I had been there when he was born, the very first person he'd seen as he lay there covered in that white gooey-looking transparent sac. It gave his midnight black coat a bluish tint. I'll never forget Dr. Showbert, the veterinarian, saying Blue was the largest colt he had ever seen. I knew from that very moment what I would call him.

"Shhhh. Big Blue, shhhh. That's it. Come on, it's okay," I coaxed in my softest persuasive voice as Big Blue inched closer to the gate and let me stroke his beautiful black face. I gently traced the white diamond on his forehead, a gesture he always seemed to love, and a bubbling thrill tingled throughout my blood when he nuzzled my cheek.

I was pleased that Blue let me pet him, but my mind seethed with anger over the prospect of Courtland Reese, a guy my own age, handling my horse. A boy Max despised. A boy who was the talk of every rancher within ten miles of Pleasant Ridge. He always seemed different from other boys, standoffish, and he looked a bit older than the rest of the guys in school. It was rumored—if you paid attention to those sorts of things—that Courtland had some weird ability to communicate with animals, particularly horses. Back in elementary school, kids made fun of him, calling him "Dr. Doolittle" and "freak." Not so much anymore though, now that we were all seniors and way too cool for such immature behavior—well, most of us. Max still referred to him as "Freakazoid." Courtland was also half Miwok Native American and most people said that was where he got his strange ability. I think a lot of the kids regarded him as scary and unapproachable more than anything else. He was quiet and didn't socialize much, which didn't help his reputation. I'd always thought he had a certain bad-boy look—sort of a leftover hot guy from that movie, "The Outsiders." Yeah, I'm an 80's movie nerd.

Certain that I could do better than Courtland, I smiled and nuzzled Big Blue right back. Courtland Reese had nothing compared to this kind of love. Big Blue was mine and nobody could ever soothe him the way I could. "See, Dad? Big Blue is fine. We don't need Courtland."

It wasn't that I didn't like Courtland. All I really knew about the guy was what Max told me. Maxen Wendell, my best friend, future boyfriend and husband, *only he didn't know it yet*, was an excellent judge when it came to sizing up people. Max was popular, always had been, just the opposite of Courtland. I sort of felt special that Max actually hung around with me ... considering I wasn't popular. Max and I became friends outside of school because we lived close to each other and I was probably the only other person his age within six miles other than Courtland.

Max said Courtland was too "sweet" so he must be a mama's boy as well as a pansy. I'd thought about pointing out that Courtland's mother died several years ago so he couldn't possibly be a mama's boy, but it really wasn't something worth starting an argument over. I wasn't even sure about the sweet part; he didn't look very sweet to me. He frowned a lot and never spoke to me unless I said something to him, which rarely ever happened, mostly because we really had nothing in common except for our love of animals. Court wasn't a bad guy. I guess I just never really took the time to get to know him, but today wasn't the day to start. I didn't want him near Big Blue, except my father seemed to think Courtland Reese had what it took to make or break a good stud like my horse.

"Well, I'm calling him anyway," my dad said, interrupting my thoughts. "There are other animals around here besides Blue that could use a bit of calming."

Convinced that Big Blue was steady and unflustered, I trucked back inside the house to help pick up china with my mom, another spirit in dire need of appeasement. Mom sniffled as she swept up shattered pieces of china and my heart felt as broken as Mom's dishes, not for the china, but for my mother. She put so much stock in preserving the past. Personally, I didn't see the importance but respected the fact that she did.

"Sorry, Mom." I didn't really know what else to say to her so I grabbed another dustpan and broom.

Angelica Castielle, the ever-protective angel, shooed me away. "Careful, honey. I'm afraid you'll cut yourself. I'll finish sweeping this up. Why don't you go help with the twins instead? Could you get them dressed and give them some cereal?" Did it bother me that my mother would, on occasion, treat me like a twelve-year-old? Yeah, but this particular time I was thankful to be away from her sniffling over broken antique porcelain.

"Sure." I forced a smile and headed toward the twins' room. I'd rather help them figure out what they were going to wear anyway. My siblings' choices of clothing never failed to amuse me. Ambrosia always wanted to mimic Aaron. She was no doubt slated to be the next great tomboy in our small town of Pleasant Ridge, following in my very own footsteps. In fact, I still wanted to do everything Max did. I'd been following him around most of my life. Max is the one and only child of Julie and Carl Wendell, owners of Wendell Winery, the second largest vineyard in Pleasant Ridge, California. My parents provided Max with free riding lessons from the time he turned ten years old. They also allowed him to board his horse Misty, a golden mare, in our stable in exchange for some great—from what I'd heard—wine. Max joked that Misty had the hots for Big Blue. Hell, he might've been right.

As I rounded the corner, I smiled at the usual banter coming from the twins' room. I paused at the doorway and shrieked when I saw Ambrosia sporting a plastic baseball bat in her hands ready to swing it at Aaron's head.

"Ambrosia, don't you dare hit Aaron with that bat! Give that to me. Do you want to put your brother in the hospital?"

Ambrosia dropped the bat as if it suddenly acquired some magical power and singed her hands. Sitting on the lower bed, she pulled the pink comforter up to her chin, and shook her head, her reddish brown curls dangling over her face and down her back. "He called me a baby because I cried when the earthcrack happened this morning," she confessed with an angelic pout.

"Earthquake," I corrected and looked at my little brother. "Aaron, I cried too. Does that make me a baby?" Well, I hadn't exactly cried, but almost and he didn't need to know that.

Aaron scrunched his eyebrows together, jumped off the bed and stood, shooting his fists straight up in the air. His identical reddish brown curls fluffed around his head, and a thin red blanket tied around his upper chest hung down his back. Mom made sure he knew never to tie anything around his neck and he took it literally. "Don't worry, I will protect you. Me and Dad. We're the mans of this family."

"Well, I feel much better now, don't you,

Ambie?" Ambrosia rolled her eyes and giggled. I'd taken to calling her that after I read in some paranormal story that ambrosia meant "food of the gods, said to bestow immortality." Picturing my little sister as some immortal's snack sort of grossed me out. My mom thought it would be cute for all of us to have the same initials as she and my dad, ARC. Actually, I thought it gave us all some sort of bond, something that connected us, more than just blood.

"Let's see, what do you guys want to wear today?"

"Mama said we didn't have school today 'cause of the earthcrack," Aaron pouted.

"Right."

"When can we go back to school?" he asked.

"Stupid earthcracks. I don't like them." Ambrosia jumped off the bed, standing stiff with her arms crossed over her chest and sticking out her bottom lip, while Aaron stood at her side, a mirror image.

"Yeah, stupid earthcracks," he mimicked.

"In about a week, I guess." I handed Aaron a pair of jeans and a blue shirt I pulled from his drawer. "Here, put these on. Ambrosia, you have a blue shirt, don't you? Oh here it is," I said, rummaging through the messy drawer that my mom would no doubt have a fit over. That is, if she ever got over the mess in the rest of the house.

"Who's here?" Aaron asked at the sound of a knock on the front door.

"Probably that obnoxious Courtland guy. Daddy wants him to help soothe the horses," I said with a sigh.

"He's not noxious. He's nice and handsome, like Daddy. I want to marry him when I grow up." Ambrosia twirled around, holding her clothes out in front of her so they flowed through the air.

"You're stupid." Aaron rolled his eyes and pounced onto his bed.

"Shhh. Both of you get dressed; I'll go tell him Daddy's in the stable."

I strolled toward the door, glancing in the living room on my way. The vacuum roared with an occasional crunching sound as my mother pushed the beast over and over the area in front of the hutch.

I opened the door to find Courtland Reese. His already broad shoulders seemed huge in that dark green hoodie zipped halfway up his chest, revealing a dark blue and black checkered shirt I'd seen him wear before. As I remembered, it had tight short sleeves that made him look rather tough the way his muscles peeked out from the hem of the sleeve, not like the freaky weird guy everyone claimed he was. He ran his fingers through his dark hair and gave me an almost dangerous looking half-smile then looked down at his feet. He shifted from one foot to the other, sticking both hands in his pockets before glancing back at me with vibrant green eyes. I don't remember ever being this close to him and I suddenly felt like I'd forgotten to get dressed. I'd never noticed his eyes before or the way they could make me feel so defenseless. He kept glancing around the front yard as if he was looking for something. Why did he always act like there were a million and one things he'd rather be doing than talking to me? Well, the feeling was mutual, I'm sure.

His dog Shiloh, on the other hand, a black mixed lab, took a step forward, wanting my attention. My heart melted as she wagged her tail fast enough to knock a small child across the porch and nuzzled the palm of my hand, her wet cold nose sliming my fingers. I smiled at the feeling and looked up into Courtland's eyes that lingered on me for a few seconds before he averted them back to the ground once again.

"Ah, is your dad home?"

I nodded, unable to find my voice. *Why was it again Max hated Courtland?*

"He called me to come over to check on the horses," Courtland said, his eyes squinting from the sun, making him frown a bit, adding to that dangerous look he sometimes had going.

Now I was the one studying the cracks in the old red-painted concrete porch my dad had been threatening to remodel with wood decking since we'd moved there eight years ago. Why anyone would paint concrete is beyond me. What's wrong with plain gray? I mean, everybody knows it's concrete.

"He's over at the stable," I said, managing to locate my voice somewhere down past my esophagus, the statement so curt, I even surprised myself.

"Thanks." He turned and headed down the pathway.

"Wait," I shouted, not sure what I wanted to say. I wasn't about to apologize for my rudeness, that's for sure, but I didn't want him to mess with Big Blue. I wanted to be the one to calm him and talk to him. Big Blue was my horse and I didn't see the need to have a stranger whisper in my horse's ear. If anybody was going to do any whispering to Big Blue, it was going to be me, no matter what my dad said.

He turned and stared at me; the cool morning breeze blew his thick dark hair into his eyes. He brushed the strands away with long slender fingers and for the first time, I noticed that his eyes were not only green but also the deepest shade of emerald I'd ever seen.

"Yeah?" he said coolly.

"Um …what exactly are you going to do?"

His lip curved up on one side. "Well, I don't know yet. I'll have to ask the horses what they want."

I blinked. "Oh," was all I could think of to say to such an odd statement and he turned and walked away. Shiloh pushed her nose against my hand one more time before turning to follow Court. *What did he mean, "ask the horses?"*

Acknowledgments

Even though this book is completely fiction, it was a difficult one to write and without the people in my life and the support they give me, I wouldn't have been able to do it. Writing *Beautifully Wounded* has been a labor of love, a story I started many years ago, on a subject no one likes to talk about. I'm glad I finally had the time and courage to give it the attention it deserved. I wanted *Beautifully Wounded* to be a romance, and tried not to undermine the seriousness of the situation.

Acknowledgments are also difficult to write, making sure everyone I love is included and not forgotten.

My first thanks is to my husband, Harry. Thank you, honey, for giving me the support and opportunity to do what I love and for reading everything I write. I'd be lost without your helpful suggestions. I also appreciate your mentioning my book to every complete stranger you meet, which embarrasses the heck out of me, but I love it and love you. You are my rock and my knight in shining armor. To my kids, for all your love and support and my Mom, for your encouragement and support and not making too many comments about my absentmindedness because my mind is usually on a character or a scene and for telling everyone you know I wrote a book.

Thank you, Michelle Olson, my editor, you are the best. You've been a huge help in bringing this book to life with all your encouraging words and praises. Thank you, Pam Ripling aka Anne Carter, for answering all my stupid questions that I constantly bug you with. A owe a special thank you to Rachael Wade for giving me the encouragement I needed to finish this story. Until you read what I'd written those many years ago, this story was nothing more than just an idea sitting on my hard drive. Love and hugs to my beta readers and awesome writer friends, Amber Garza, Tina Donnelly, Pam Ripling, Kate Givens, and Derinda Love, thank you for your insightful suggestions, you helped pull this book together. And a special thank you to my awesome Personal Assistant, Tina Donnelly, you are making my life easier every day and I am proud to call you my sister.

To you, the reader, you own my heart, because without you, this story would be sitting on my hard drive collecting cyber dust. Thank you for reading.

About Susan Griscom

I grew up in a small town in Pennsylvania, spending most of my time daydreaming or playing around in the mud. I grew out of the mud play, well, most of the time, a good soak in the mud is always fun. I still daydream often and sometimes my daydreams interrupt my daydreams. So I write to remember them. If I didn't write, I think my mind would explode from an overload of fantasy and weirdness. To the annoyance of my friends and family, my characters sometimes become a part of my world. During my childhood, I would frequently get in trouble in school for daydreaming. Eventually, my vivid imagination paid off and I had the privilege of writing and co-directing my sixth-grade class play--a dreadful disaster, though not from my writing, of course. I'm pretty sure it was the acting.

I enjoy writing about characters living in small quaint towns and tend to lean toward the unusual and edgy.

My paranormal playing field delves into a different milieu, abandoning vampires and werewolves, but not discounting them. Someday I might like to write a novel about vamps and those furry creatures. But for now I like the bizarre mixed with romance. A strong hero or heroine confronted with extraordinary forces of nature, powers and capabilities gets my blood running hot, as does a steamy contemporary romantic suspense.

Find out more about Susan Griscom by visiting her website.

http://susangriscom.com

Facebook: http://www.facebook.com/SMGriscom
Follow Susan on Twitter:
https://twitter.com/SusanGriscom

If you've enjoyed reading *Beautifully Wounded*, please take a moment to write a review on sites such as Amazon, Barnes and Noble, or Goodreads

Made in the USA
Charleston, SC
13 June 2014